Reid

Reid and Tara

The Davenports

Book Three

SJ McCoy

A Sweet n Steamy Romance

Published by Xenion, Inc

Reid. Copyright © SJ McCoy 2018

Published by Xenion, Inc.
First Paperback edition October 2018
www.sjmccoy.com

Cover Design by Dana Lamothe of Designs by Dana
Editor: Mitzi Pummer Carroll
Proofreaders: Aileen Blomberg and Marisa Nichols

ISBN 978-1-946220-43-1

Dedication

For Sam. Sometimes, life really is too short. Few.

xxx

Chapter One

"I can cancel the appointment, Nicole. I can go some other time."

"You've been saying that for months. If you carry on at this rate, you won't have used your gift certificate by the time your next birthday rolls around. Go. Please. Owen will be fine here."

Tara blew out a sigh. She wasn't so sure about that. He did okay with his Aunt Nicole, but the girls stressed him out.

Nicole knew why she was so reluctant. "I'll make the girls play in their room. Owen can stay with me. I promise. I won't let them upset him. You need to go. You never do anything for yourself. When I bought you this massage, I was hoping that you might make it a regular thing, that you'd go once a week, or even once a month. You need some pampering. All you ever do is work and take care of Owen."

"He needs me."

"I know he does, but you need to take care of yourself, too. You need to have a life, even if it is only for an hour here and there."

Tara looked at her watch. If she didn't leave soon, she'd miss the appointment anyway.

Her sister gave her a shrewd look. "I know damned well what you're thinking; that if you drag it out long enough, it'll be too

late for you to go and you can just skip it. Think again. You're
going to get your ass into that cab and leave. Now."

Tara looked over at Owen. He was engrossed in his dinosaur
book.

"Go," insisted Nicole. "If you say goodbye to him, you'll only
upset him, and then you'll never get out of here. He'll be fine.
I promise."

Tara nodded reluctantly. "Okay, but only if you promise me
you'll call if something sets him off."

"He'll be fine."

"Promise me, or I'm not going."

"Okay, okay. I promise." Nicole smiled. "Sister's honor."

Tara chuckled. "All right. I'll be back as soon as I can."

"Take your time. We'll see you later."

Tara had second thoughts as soon as she'd given the cab
driver the name of the hotel. Just saying the name of the place
felt wrong. It wasn't like her to go to a fancy place like that for
a massage. She wasn't one of those women who spent her days
getting mani-pedis and doing lunch. She was an elementary
school teacher; well, she wasn't even one of those anymore.
She was a work-at-home freelancer whose life revolved around
her son. And that was as it should be. Owen was her world.
He was special. She gladly dedicated her life to making his
bearable. She blew out a sigh, and the cab driver met her gaze
in the rearview mirror.

"Everything all right?"

She nodded, wanting to tell him to turn around and go back.
Nicole would be so mad at her if she went back now. And she
would call if Owen needed her. She took her phone out of her
purse to make sure the volume was turned all the way up—just
in case.

She felt self-conscious as she walked through the lobby. She
should have gotten dressed up. Her shorts and flip-flops set

her apart from all the business suits and designer-casual outfits sported by other guests. Even the staff in their elegant uniforms looked like they were from a different league—because they were.

She drew in a deep breath as the woman at the concierge desk smiled politely at her. "Good afternoon. How may I help you?"

At least the question hadn't been what the hell do you think you're doing in here? Tara forced herself to smile back. "I have an appointment at the spa."

"I'll call them for you and have someone come out to take you through."

"Thanks." Tara couldn't help but wonder if that was the usual procedure or if the woman just didn't want someone who looked the way she did wandering around the premises unaccompanied.

"Take a seat." The woman gestured to one of the plush white leather sofas.

Tara sat down and picked up a magazine. She needed to relax. That was the whole point of coming here, to have a little time to herself and de-stress. She made herself breathe deeply as she flicked through the pages, but she couldn't focus. The pictures weren't as interesting as the patrons of the hotel. She watched two women who were arriving back from a shopping trip—as evidenced by the bellhop following them with an assortment of bags bearing the names Hermes, Gucci, and a couple more. The women chatted happily as they sauntered confidently toward the elevators. Tara had to wonder about their lives. Were they on vacation? Was this a girl's trip away or just a day out? Did they have children? She made herself stop there. She didn't need to know. Even if they did have kids, she was sure there were no comparisons to be drawn.

She turned her attention to the check-in desk. Whoa! She dropped her gaze and wanted to fan herself. She'd just locked eyes with the sexiest man she'd ever seen in real life. There was heat in her cheeks. She could feel it; she just hoped no one could see it. She lifted her gaze without raising her head, wanting to check him out without it being obvious. She needn't have worried. He was talking to the woman behind the desk, handing over his card. He was either checking in or out. For a crazy moment, she hoped he was checking in, that he wasn't leaving—but it didn't matter in the slightest. It wasn't like she'd ever see him again even if he was checking in and staying for a month.

He was panty-dropping gorgeous. She smiled at the expression. It wasn't one she'd used or even thought about in years—probably not since she'd had Owen. It was, nevertheless, the most appropriate way to describe the guy. He was tall, broad-shouldered, though not overly so. He was more athletic looking than muscular. Just her type. As if she had a type anymore. There was a mysterious air to him. He had the chiseled jaw and the aristocratic features. He could be a wealthy, confident businessman, but something about him said he wasn't a businessman or a playboy. He was something else! That was the only way to describe him. Her heart was pounding as she watched him. He smiled at the woman checking him in, but he wasn't overly friendly or jovial. She smiled at the thought that maybe he was a spy, some international man of mystery who wanted to go unnoticed. She doubted he'd be able to pull that off looking the way he did.

"Hi there. I'm Amanda from Bliss. Are you the lady waiting to come for your appointment?"

Tara jumped at the interruption to her musings about mystery man and looked up with an embarrassed smile, even though the girl standing there couldn't know what she'd been up to.

"I am. The name's Tara Wilder."

"Great. I thought that must be you. Would you like to come with me?"

Tara got to her feet and shot one last look back at mystery man. Bad timing. He'd finished checking in and was walking toward her. His gaze locked with hers. Green eyes. Her heart raced again. She loved green eyes. He stopped walking and just stood there staring at her. She smiled, but he didn't smile back. He looked puzzled as if he thought he recognized her but couldn't place her.

"Shall we?" Amanda from the spa gave her a puzzled look.

"Yes. Of course. I'm sorry." Tara scurried after her. She had to pull herself together. Mystery man had probably been puzzled about what someone dressed like her was even doing here. He might call a manager to have her thrown out if she didn't scoot.

They walked through a lush tropical garden on their way to the spa. Amanda gave her a curious look. "Forgive me for asking …"

Tara tensed, wondering what was coming.

"Was that someone you know?"

"Oh." So, she hadn't imagined the way mystery man had looked at her. "No."

Amanda smiled. "That's a shame. I wish I knew him." She giggled. "You know what I mean."

Tara giggled with her, glad to relieve the tension. "Oh, I know exactly what you mean."

"We get some good-looking guys who come through here, but he's the sexiest I've seen so far."

"I chose a good day then."

"You did. Although, if you buy the package, I'm sure you'll see some eye candy any time you come."

"The package?"

Amanda looked over her shoulder. "Yeah, don't be surprised if they lay it on thick while you're in there. They just introduced a new commission system, and my manager has us all trying to sell packages to everyone who comes through the door."

"Well, they're wasting their time with me. This is a one-off gift certificate deal."

"I thought as much; that's why I wanted to warn you."

"Thanks." Tara didn't need to ask why Amanda thought that. It was obvious she wasn't part of their target market.

"I'm sorry. I didn't mean that to come out wrong. I was trying to look out for you, not put you down."

"Thanks. I appreciate it. I'm just feeling a little out of place."

"Well, don't. You've paid the same as everyone else who walks through the door for a massage. I wasn't putting you down, don't you put yourself down either."

Tara smiled. "You're right. I've paid the same—at least, my sister did—and I have no doubt I've earned it."

Amanda smiled back as they reached the spa. "I don't either. You deserve this, I can tell. Make the most of it and enjoy it."

~ ~ ~

Reid watched the girl in the denim shorts walk away. He wanted to stop her, but there was nothing he could do. Sometimes, he wished he were more like his brother, Oscar. Oscar wouldn't have hesitated. He would have followed those long legs, caught up with her, chatted with her, charmed her—and before the afternoon was over, would no doubt have screwed her and forgotten her name, if he ever took the time to ask for it. No. Reid was no Oscar. He reached up and straightened his collar. He wouldn't want to be.

He looked around, feeling a little self-conscious. He must have been standing here for over a minute. That girl—she'd caught him off guard. He didn't normally react like this. He was used to beautiful women. They tended to throw themselves at him—a perk of his family name, and in some cases, a perk of his work. Admittedly there were more beautiful women eager to sleep with a wealthy Davenport brother than there were who knew about his tech prowess, though there were some. He doubted he'd ever get to sleep with a groupie of his sci-fi writing alter-ego, who went by the pen name Rupert Raines.

He made his way to the elevators and headed up to his room. He wanted to take a shower and change before he went to see TJ. He doubted he'd ever see the beautiful redhead with the big, blue eyes and the long, long legs again, let alone get to sleep with her. He met his own gaze in the mirrored wall of the elevator. He didn't like to admit it to himself, but attractive as she was, much as his body had reacted to her physically, sleeping with her hadn't been his main consideration. She'd looked like someone he wanted to know. He pursed his lips. That was an illogical conclusion to draw. There was no way he could ascertain whether she was someone whose company he would enjoy. Yet, somehow, he knew it was true.

His bags had reached his room before he did. That was one of the reasons he stayed here whenever he came to LA: efficiency. It was important to him. He went through to the bathroom and washed his hands. He couldn't help smiling as he dried them. Soft towels: they were another reason he stayed here. Scratchy towels weren't something he wanted to deal with. He could—if he had to—but over the years, he'd learned to arrange his affairs so he didn't have to deal with many of the stressors that had made his early life so challenging.

He went back through the living room area and stood by the window, taking in the view. In many respects, LA was not his favorite city. He couldn't live here, but he dealt with it. He dealt with it because it was where both his brothers lived. Oscar, who to be fair, had now ended his womanizing ways for the sake of his cool fiancée, Grace, and TJ. Reid had been worried about TJ for a while after he returned to the States. He'd served in Afghanistan and had lost many of his friends over there. Reid had come down here every weekend to stay with him at first, but he'd come a long way since then—to the point where he'd recently gotten engaged.

That was the purpose of this visit—to meet TJ's new fiancée, Dani. At least, as far as his brothers were concerned, that was the purpose. For Reid, there was a dual purpose. His brothers had become very involved in running a community center, and according to his mom, their latest endeavor was a book drive. They were collecting books from the community for the vets and the homeless and the kids who came to the center. His mom had chatted on about how one of the vets had come up with the idea because reading was such a great escape. That had struck a chord with Reid—reading had always been one of his escape routes. He wanted to contribute, to be a part of it, and since neither TJ nor Oscar had mentioned it to him, he'd taken matters into his own hands. And that was the dual purpose of his visit.

His cell phone rang, and he fished it out of his pocket. It was TJ.

"Yes. I'm here. I'm at the hotel."

TJ chuckled. "I'll never train you to answer with hello, will I?"

"No. It's inefficient. You didn't call to say hello. You called to see if I'm in town yet, and your next question will probably be what time and where are we meeting up. I don't have enough information on your plans or whereabouts, and I have no other calls on my time. So, logically, you should tell me where and when."

TJ chuckled again. "Okay. Do you want to come to the house at seven? Dani and I are still at the center, and we're going to be a while."

"Okay. I'll see you at seven. Can I bring anything?"

"No. It's all good. Dani's trying her hand at hosting."

"I thought she didn't cook?"

"So did she. She has the numbers for a couple of caterers ready in case it's a disaster, but she wants to give it a try."

Reid smiled. He liked that idea.

"Why silent? I know you. You're either pleased or displeased. Which is it?"

"I'm pleased. It means she doesn't consider me to be someone distant who must be formally impressed."

TJ laughed. "Yep, you're probably right there. She's excited to meet you. She read your books, and she loves them."

"She did?"

"Yeah, she wanted to get to know you; that was the only way she could till you came."

"I'm glad she wanted to. I'll see you at seven."

"Yep. See you then."

Reid hung up and smiled to himself. He already liked the sound of Dani, and she'd received resounding endorsements from his parents and from Oscar and Grace. The fact that she'd read his books made him like her a little more. Neither of his brothers had read them, he was sure of that.

He checked his watch. He had a few hours to kill. He could get some work done on his laptop. He had admin details to catch up on, but he didn't particularly want to. He stared out the window again, taking in the city skyline, appreciating the precise angles, if not the haze and smog. What did he want to do? He pressed his lips together, trying to suppress a smile. He wanted to go back down to the lobby to see if he might spot the redhead with the long legs again. It was silly, he knew, but he also knew that it was good to be silly sometimes. Life got boring when everything was too precisely planned and managed. He liked to introduce elements of chance and randomness occasionally. This could be one of those occasions.

As he rode back down in the elevator, he was eighty percent sure that he wouldn't see her again, and ninety percent sure that he'd do nothing more than observe if he did. He wasn't above meeting a woman and taking her home—to her place or back to a hotel room. But he still had that same feeling about her. He wanted to know the woman with the blue eyes and long legs, not just pick her up.

The doors opened, and he looked around as he stepped out into the lobby. Of course, there was no sign of her. He made his way over to the bar area and took up a perch on the very end stool. He already knew that it was optimally positioned to observe the entire lobby. From here he could see the main entrance, the elevators, and the doors to the garden and pool through which she'd disappeared earlier.

A waiter arrived with a smile. "It's good to see you, Mr. Davenport. Can I get you the usual?"

"Please, Tony."

Tony returned a few minutes later and placed a fresh pineapple juice in front of him.

Reid raised an eyebrow.

Tony smiled. "Don't worry. I heard that you checked in a little while ago, so I made some fresh for you."

"Thanks." Once Tony had gone, Reid let his gaze flit around the lobby. He wasn't looking for her, just observing the patrons and staff. He knew the uniforms and what they designated. The front desk staff wore royal blue jackets with white shirts, the bellhops wore mustard yellow and those stupid little hats—it wasn't the 1800s, for God's sake. The concierge staff wore a cream-colored outfit with navy piping. Reid sipped his juice and thought about it. The girl who had come to collect the redhead had been minus navy piping. He frowned. That was a detail that had eluded him until now. Her piping had been pink. He smiled to himself, grateful that his thoughts didn't appear in a bubble over his head for anyone to read. Her piping had been pink—and therefore, she worked at the spa. He didn't frequent the place, but they touted their services aggressively, and their brochures always featured employees wearing cream suits with pink piping.

Great. So, was he going to make a visit to the spa? No. She would have an appointment and no doubt be in a private room somewhere. The appointment would last a minimum of an hour. Judging by her attire, she wouldn't be there for multiple treatments. He'd guess one hour and no more. If he was right, she'd be out in forty minutes or so and he'd get a glimpse of her and ... who knew? If he was wrong, then at least he'd have killed some time before he went to TJ's.

Chapter Two

Tara watched the masseuse's feet through the hole in the table. She was trying her hardest to relax, but it wasn't working too well. The hot stones had been bliss—just as the name of this place promised—but she wasn't big on having someone's hands all over her. She closed her eyes and indulged in the thought that she wouldn't mind having mystery man's hands on her. She didn't know what had come over her. She hadn't had the time, energy, or interest to think about a man that way in years. She got a little too involved in some of the romance novels she edited, but book boyfriends were the only kind she'd had since she and Mark had divorced. If Owen's father hadn't been able to handle him, how on earth could she expect any other man to? No. Owen was the only guy in her life, and she expected that wouldn't change for many years—if ever. She didn't know how Owen would cope as he got older. Some people claimed that autistic kids could develop the life skills that would enable them to make their own way in the world. Tara wasn't so sure. If Owen needed her until the day she died, then he would be her number one priority.

She let out a sigh as the masseuse's palms worked their way up her spine. Since she was unlikely to have a real man in her life, there was no harm in indulging in a little fantasy—not when she'd just seen such a fantasy-inspiring guy. She closed her eyes again and pictured mystery man's handsome face, and his green eyes focused on her.

Both she and the masseuse jumped when her cell phone started to ring.

"I'm sorry, but we don't allow those in the treatment rooms."

Tara was already scrambling up from the table, trying to cover herself with the towel as she went. "I know, but I have to have it. It's on silent for everyone but my sister who's minding my son."

The masseuse didn't look impressed. "You can't take calls in here."

"I have to."

"Then I'm afraid this appointment—"

"What's up, Nicole?"

"I'm really sorry. The girls took his dinosaur and ..."

Tara could hear Owen freaking out in the background. "I'll call a cab right now. I'll be back as soon as I can."

"Just come out and meet us. We're almost there. All he wants is his momma. I thought it best to bring him to you."

"Okay. I'll get dressed and meet you out front." Tara shrugged at the masseuse. "You're right. This appointment is over."

Reid sipped his drink and let his gaze flit around the lobby. It was full of the usual suspects. No sign of the redhead yet, but then he didn't really expect there to be. His drink was almost gone, and he was starting to think that this was a bad idea. He wanted to catch a glimpse of her, but other than that, he didn't know why he was here. If he wanted to see her, he'd have to order another drink which he didn't want. He'd probably just watch her walk through the lobby, and that would be it. It wasn't a logical way to spend his time. He looked up at the sound of a child shouting. It was a small boy coming in through the main entrance. He was holding the hand of a very flustered looking woman who was probably in her early thirties.

All heads had turned in the direction of the commotion. Reid blew out a sigh. He didn't need to witness this. He felt bad for the young mother and for the child. He waved at Tony that he was leaving. It meant he'd miss the redhead if she came back through, but so be it. Cost-benefit exercise; since he had no plan to do anything more than catch a glimpse of her, the benefit didn't outweigh the cost of witnessing a small child's distress and the mother's discomfort and embarrassment.

He hesitated on his way back to the elevator. Was he ready to give up on the chance of another sight of her? No. He was surprised at his answer, but no, he still had a little hope of seeing her. Perhaps if he paid a visit to the men's room— which he needed to do anyway—the child would be gone, and he could order another drink and while away a little more time. When he emerged from the men's room, the shouts of the child could still be heard. He was sitting on one of the sofas behind the concierge desk—out of the way, as much as possible. The woman with him … wasn't the one who'd brought him in. It was the redhead! What kind of irony was that? The small person who'd driven him away was now with the woman who'd drawn him out here. He blew out a sigh and approached the concierge desk. There was no one sitting there, and hopefully, they wouldn't come scurrying out to attend to him too quickly.

The child was frantic. He was shouting and lashing out at the redhead. She seemed calm, if harried. She kept looking around as if she expected someone to come and ask them to leave. Reid was sure that someone would when they figured out that she wasn't a guest. He felt bad for her. She was in an unenviable situation.

In general, he preferred to avoid unnecessary social contact, but he made certain exceptions; if he could help, then he'd step in. He had a feeling, judging by the child's actions, that he might be able to help in this case. And since he'd been hoping for some form of social contact with the woman—whom he now assumed to be the mother—then what harm was there?

He patted his jacket pocket, glad he was still wearing it. He believed that what he had in there could be the solution.

The redhead looked up as he approached. Her eyes widened. She wasn't afraid of him; it was recognition. He'd guess that he'd had a similar effect on her earlier to the one she'd had on him—perhaps that was more of a hope than a guess.

The child began to rock again and redoubled his screaming.

"It's okay. Owen. They've gone. You have your dinosaur. Aunt Nicole gave it back to you, and she's taken the girls home now. It's just us. When you calm down, we can take a taxi and go home."

The child screamed again.

Reid noted that the redhead wasn't hugging him or making any attempt to touch or hold him. Which further confirmed his suspicion about what the problem might be.

"We can go home when you calm down. The driver won't let us in a taxi while you're like this."

Reid made his way toward them. He'd seen and heard enough to believe he could help.

He didn't get a chance to speak before the redhead turned to glare at him. "I'm sorry if this is inconvenient for you. I apologize for disturbing your peace, but please don't tell me how to handle him. He doesn't need to be told off or smacked or whatever kind of firm approach you're about to suggest. You don't understand, so please don't judge. We'll be out of here sooner if you leave us alone."

Reid braced himself against the force of her words. He didn't back off, though. He just nodded and smiled. "I could be wrong, but I think I do understand. And I have a suggestion …"

Her eyes flashed with anger, but he continued to smile as he reached into his pocket and pulled out his iPod.

She gave him a puzzled look.

"Classical music. Baroque, to be precise."

She looked at him as though he might be crazy. Maybe he was, but the child made the decision for them. He reached out for the iPod. Reid looked at the redhead, and she nodded.

Reid sat down beside the boy. "Do you want to hear this?" He held the earbuds toward him.

The kid nodded and took them, pushing them into his little ears.

Reid pressed play and hoped for the best. Both he and the redhead watched the kid. Reid half expected he might pull the earphones out and get back to screaming before the music had a chance to work its magic. He was relieved when the kid wriggled back and leaned his head against the sofa. After a few moments, he started to smile and then started to move to the music.

The redhead covered her mouth with her hand. He could see her eyes were glistening with tears.

"What's he listening to?"

"Bach."

"Seriously?"

"Yes. Classical music, baroque in particular, can soothe the mind by …" He shook his head. It didn't matter. She probably didn't want or need to know the why. People were like that. They didn't care about the whys; they only wanted the benefits. He looked at the kid who was sitting still now, smiling as he moved his head in time to the melody.

"Thank you, so much. I'm sorry I snapped at you. I'm just so used to people getting all angry and judgmental. They don't understand."

"No, they don't," agreed Reid.

"That sounds like the voice of experience." She met his gaze. "Do you have an autistic child?"

"No. I don't have kids." She hadn't asked how he understood, only if he had a child. That answer was all she needed.

She held his gaze for a moment longer, but the boy edged toward her and rested his head against her arm. "Oh, wow. He's getting sleepy! That's amazing. Thank you. It normally takes hours to calm him down from an episode like this. I need to call a cab and get us out of here."

"The doorman can get you one. I'll go and have a word with him, if you want?"

When she smiled, her big blue eyes shimmered with tears. "Thank you."

He nodded.

"Do you want me to carry him out there?"

"Thanks, but he won't let you touch him."

Reid smiled and held his arms out to the kid. Big blue eyes, just like his mom's, looked up at him and then the little guy reached up and climbed into Reid's lap.

He got to his feet and smiled at the redhead who shook her head in disbelief. "Damn! I don't know who you are or what you are, but I wish there were more of you in the world."

Reid smiled. "Sorry. I'm a limited edition, one of a kind."

She nodded. "Of course, you are."

Reid wasn't surprised to see that the doorman had a cab waiting for them when they reached the front doors.

She got in first, and he reluctantly handed the child to her. The little guy clung to him for a moment.

"Thank you again. I can't thank you enough."

He smiled and shrugged. "It was nothing." It was certainly nothing like he'd expected or hoped for. But he knew that, for her, and for the kid, it had been huge.

"Where to, lady? I'm blocking everyone here."

The redhead gave Reid a sad smile. "I guess this is goodbye."

He nodded. He guessed it was, too, since he'd totally wasted the opportunity for it to be anything else. "Bach, Handel, Vivaldi, their music will all have that effect."

"Where are we going, lady?" The cab driver was getting pissed.

"You'd better go." Reid closed the cab door and watched it pull hurriedly out of the crowded drop-off lane. He made his way back inside and rode the elevator back up to his room. Once he was there, he washed his hands again, and while he dried them on the soft towel, he looked himself in the eye. "For a smart guy, that was a dumb move."

He could have asked her name, her number, found a way to see her again, to get to know her—and to see little Owen again—he didn't want to examine his reasoning behind that last one too closely. But it didn't matter anyway. He hadn't done a thing, other than watch them and the chance to get to know them, ride out of his life in the back of a cab—with his iPod. He smiled at that. Could that be viewed as a legitimate reason to track her down? His smile faded—only if he were an asshole. Who'd hunt a woman down to get an iPod back? Not him.

~ ~ ~

Tara fixed herself an iced coffee in the kitchen, focusing on every detail of the little ritual. It calmed her, and after the way this afternoon had worked out, she needed calming. At least they were home now. Owen was settled in his room working on his dinosaur puzzle. She went and leaned in his doorway. Her eyes and her heart filled up at the sight of him. He was sitting on the floor holding a puzzle piece, his little brow furrowed in concentration as he tried to work out where it went. He smiled as he slotted it into place and then sat back and began to sway. It wasn't his upset kind of rocking. No. He was swaying to the music, which she couldn't hear, but that still filled his little ears through the headphones of mystery man's iPod.

She shook her head. Mystery man had been a real knight in shining armor coming to her rescue like that. She wished she hadn't snarled at him before he'd had a chance to speak, but she was too used to people judging her when Owen went off like that. They thought he was misbehaving and weren't afraid to tell her so. She'd heard too many times from too many strangers that he needed a firmer hand, that he should be punished, that she was a bad mother. Most of the time it didn't bother her; people were ignorant and opinionated—if you let that get to you, then you didn't stand any chance of being happy in life! It had bothered her when she'd believed mystery man was about to place himself amongst the ranks of the judgmental assholes, so she'd gone on the defensive—and she couldn't have been more wrong. He'd been understanding; he'd calmed Owen; he'd saved her. She shook her head. He'd been a shining star in a very dark situation. But now the situation was behind her, and so was he. She sighed. Oh well.

The phone rang, and she went back to the kitchen to answer it. "Hello?"

"Hey, it's only me," said Nicole. "Did you get him home all right? I'm so sorry I had to just leave you there with him, but with Steve and the kids in the car …"

"Don't apologize! I'm just glad you brought him to me."

"I know, but it can't have been easy with him in the hotel lobby like that. I don't know how you handle it. I wanted the floor to open and swallow me up just to get me away from all those snooty, judgy looks we were getting. I feel so bad that I abandoned you to face it by yourself."

"Seriously, don't worry about it. I'm used to it."

"I know. And I hate that for you. It's so unfair."

"It is, but like I said, I'm used to it."

"Is he okay now?"

"He's fine. He's listening to Bach."

"Huh? You mean, like classical music? Since when is he into that?"

Tara had to smile. "Since a handsome stranger came to our rescue in the lobby after you left. He was gorgeous, Nic. He came over to where we were sitting, and Owen freaking out didn't faze him at all. He gave him his iPod, and it calmed him right down."

"Did you get his number?"

Tara laughed. "No. It wasn't like that. He was just being kind. He seemed to understand Owen. He knew what to do, he knew the music would calm him down—and he was right. Owen even let him carry him out front. He put us in a cab, and that was it."

"Owen liked him, and you didn't get his number? Damn, girl!"

"If it's any consolation, I kicked myself all the way home. I had the perfect excuse and everything. He let Owen leave with his iPod; I should have asked for his number so I could return it."

Nicole blew out a big sigh. "You're breaking my heart here, sis. You meet a guy, a guy who's kind, who's good to both you and Owen, and you let him slip through your fingers."

"Yeah, well. It's not like I could date him anyway. This afternoon was proof that I can't leave Owen."

"Don't say that. I'm sorry the girls got his dinosaur, and it set him off. They weren't being mean, they were just trying to play with him."

"I know. I wasn't complaining or criticizing. It's just how it is. If he's not with me, he's not right. And it's not fair to ask you to take him. You've got enough on your plate with the girls. They don't understand. They just want to play."

"I just hate it for you. You need to be able to go somewhere without him, sometimes. You can't spend your entire life with him twenty-four-seven."

"I can, and I do. It is what it is. I wouldn't change it. He needs me."

Nicole was quiet for a few moments.

"I know what you're thinking, but no. He doesn't need to go to one of those groups. He's not ready."

"He's not, or you're not?"

"Drop it, Nic. He's not going, so us fighting about it is pointless."

"Okay. I'm sorry. I just have to bring it up every now and then, see if your thinking's changed."

"It hasn't and it won't."

"Okay. Topic closed. And just so we leave things on a happier note, tell me about your handsome stranger?"

Tara smiled. She'd be happy to. "He was gorgeous! I'd seen him checking in while I was waiting for my appointment. It was one of those—our eyes met across a crowded room—moments."

"What did he look like? What was he wearing?"

"Black suit, white shirt. Dark hair, green eyes. He was just … yummy! There's no other word for him."

"Suit? Like a business suit? You think he's here on business? Was there a ring?"

Tara's smile disappeared. "I don't know. I didn't check for a ring." A ball of disappointment settled in the pit of her stomach. She knew it was crazy. What did it matter either way? She'd never see him again.

"Just pretend there was no ring. I know you, you'll get all upset that he's probably married—and he's just a nice fantasy, so it doesn't matter."

"I'm a step ahead of you. I just figured that out. So, no, I don't think he's married, and no, I don't think he's a businessman either. I can tell you, you'll laugh at me, but then you always do. I was thinking that maybe he was a spy or something. He wasn't one of those look-at-me types. He was obviously wealthy and confident, but he wasn't all outgoing. I'd decided he was an international man of mystery, maybe a spy like in the movies. He's just here on an assignment and is trying to keep a low profile."

Nicole laughed. "You shouldn't just edit books, you should write them. You make up awesome stories for the people you see."

Tara nodded. "I've been thinking about doing that."

"You should. You could write romances and at least that way you'd have some kind of love life."

"Ha. Thanks. That's what I was thinking, too."

"Well, if you won't leave Owen with me and start dating, it's about your only option."

"I know, and I'm okay with it."

"Okay. I'll stop nagging, then. Call me tomorrow?"

"Okay. Will do.

"Bye."

Tara hung up and went back to check on Owen. He was still swaying happily to the music. She decided to get online and see what other baroque music she could download for him—and of course, she needed to research how and why it had the effect it did. It was great that it helped, but she needed to understand the why of it.

Chapter Three

"Are you sure it's edible?"

Reid had to laugh at the look on Dani's face as she watched him eat. She obviously didn't believe that he was enjoying the meal she'd prepared. He was. The food, like the rest of the evening so far, was enjoyable. It was easy to relax with TJ and Dani, especially sitting out here, in their back yard dining al fresco by the pool. "It's delicious," he said with a smile. "The only thing I would change would be to add more garlic, but I'm only telling you because you demanded one hundred percent honest feedback."

He was relieved when she smiled. In his experience, women often insisted that you tell them the truth, then overreacted and took it badly when you did.

"That's good to know, thanks. I almost put more in, but I stuck with what the recipe called for since I'm a garlic fiend."

TJ smiled and put a hand on her shoulder. "I told you, you don't need to worry. Mom raised us all the same way—we don't do fake nice. If it was terrible, we'd tell you." He smirked at Reid. "Wouldn't we?"

Reid nodded at Dani. "He's right. All three of us are the same. Mom drilled it into us that we should be polite, but honest. I sometimes take it a little further than he and Oscar do because I don't always remember to factor in people's emotions."

TJ laughed. "You can't factor them in when they don't make sense to you."

Dani put her fork down and gave Reid a puzzled look. "Emotions don't make sense?"

Reid shrugged. "They do when I stop and think about them. At least, I can run them through my internal database of experience and observation and figure out why and how I just made someone cry."

Dani was genuinely interested, he could tell. "So, you don't feel things yourself?"

He nodded slowly. "I do, but not in the way other people seem to. Emotions seem … inefficient. They crop up out of nowhere and mostly they're irrelevant to whatever I'm trying to achieve. For me, personally, I can just brush them aside, and if there's anything left of them later, I'll sort through them. It seems a more normal way to do things is to let emotions derail you. People need to stop and deal with them before they can reach their objective—in any endeavor."

TJ chuckled and looked at Dani. "And by the way, yes, he always sounds as though he swallowed a dictionary."

Dani pushed at his arm. "I'm a journalist, remember. I appreciate a man who can use words eloquently."

Reid laughed as TJ scowled at her. "Hey. I'm eloquent when I want to be."

"Yeah, about as eloquent as a bear can be."

It made Reid happy to see them together. Dani was good for TJ. Reid hadn't seen him laugh and joke like this in far too long.

"So, I'm guessing you won't mind if I ask you a personal question then—but tell me to butt out if I'm being too nosey."

"Go ahead."

"What about in relationships? I mean, we women tend to be more emotional than men, in general. And I know, for me, at least, I want a man to understand me—and my feelings. How does that work for you?"

TJ shot her a warning look, but Reid smiled. "I don't need to tell you to butt out." He nodded at TJ, wanting him to know that it really was okay. "If I'm honest, it's good to be able to talk about it. I don't tend to have many relationships."

TJ raised an eyebrow at him.

"At least, I don't tend to get involved in long-term relationships."

Dani's eyes widened. "You're not another Oscar, are you? I wouldn't have had you down as the fuck 'em and forget 'em type."

Reid laughed out loud. "No. I'm not Oscar."

"But ..." TJ held his gaze.

"But my relationships do tend to be short. And mostly ... physical."

Dani shook her head. "You surprise me."

Reid cocked his head to one side. "Why?"

"I don't know. I thought you'd be ... I don't know."

Reid smiled. "You thought I'd be the blundering geek who doesn't know how to be around women?"

She shrugged, looking a little embarrassed. "I guess, sort of, but I also kind of thought you'd be into the deep and meaningful."

"I'd like to be, one day." He took a slug of his beer and looked up at the last of the setting sun. He'd wondered about the deep and meaningful as he watched Owen and his mom ride away in that cab this afternoon. "But, I haven't met anyone yet."

TJ chuckled. "Well, maybe your time is coming. We're falling like dominoes. First Oscar, now me; maybe it's your turn soon."

Reid shrugged. He doubted that.

"In the meantime, I think you do all right with your sexy geek deal. Shane taught you well."

Reid smiled at the mention of his childhood friend. He hadn't spoken to Shane in a couple of years, but he'd heard he was settled down and married now.

"Who's Shane?" asked Dani.

"You know. I introduced you to him last time we were up in Montana. He runs the guest ranch where we ride."

"Oh! That Shane?" She looked at Reid. "What did he teach you?"

Reid smiled again at the memories that came flooding back. "You can probably figure it out for yourself. You've met Shane, and you've met me. He's big and bold and full of charm and confidence. I'm quiet and reserved and ..." He shrugged. "It wasn't the most likely friendship you could imagine."

TJ grinned. "No, but it was awesome. You should come up there and see him sometime."

"I should. It'd be good to see him again."

"Come on," said Dani. "You have to fill me in. I'm fascinated by how the two of you became friends and what he taught you."

"You know we grew up there?"

She nodded.

"But we didn't go to school there. We were homeschooled. But we used to go to social events and some of the after-school clubs. I'm sure it won't surprise you to hear that I was in the chess club."

Dani smiled and nodded for him to continue.

"Well, there was a girl who came to chess club. Tricia Conley. Shane had a crush on her, and he asked me to teach him how to play so he could come to club and play with her."

TJ laughed. "I think he did more playing with her behind the old barn than he ever did in chess club."

"I believe you're right." Reid smiled at Dani. "Shane was a good guy, even then. He had a sense of honor and fairness. He didn't think it was right that I should help him without him doing something for me in return. He asked what I wanted him to do for me. I told him I was fine, but he wouldn't take no for an answer. I couldn't think of anything, so he gave me two options. He'd teach me to ride and rope, or he'd teach me a thing or two about girls and how to make them like me. I already knew how to ride and didn't see myself ever needing to become a cowboy, so I opted for learning about girls."

"And he taught you well," said TJ.

Reid smirked at him and then straightened his face as he looked at Dani.

"Wow! That's awesome. I love that story. The geek and the cowboy helping each other out. I wish life was like that more of the time. It seems these days kids only stay with their own kind; they're more likely to bully or fight someone who's different from them than they are to help them and learn from each other."

Reid blew out a sigh. "That's true, but then look at the examples they have to learn from. Adults aren't interested in learning from or helping each other either. These days it seems most people are only interested in being right—and in proving anyone who disagrees with them wrong."

Dani and TJ both nodded sadly, making him realize that he'd taken a fun moment and turned it somber—spoiled the mood of their evening that had been going so well. He liked Dani. He was happy for TJ that he'd found her. He wanted to see them smile again—and to continue building a bond. "Sorry. Sometimes the way the world is gets me down; that's why I try to avoid it mostly. However, can we go back to where we were? Talking about me and how I do or don't fare with women?"

"Sure." TJ looked puzzled, no doubt surprised that he wanted to open up.

Dani nodded eagerly.

"I had an encounter today. I don't know what to do about it. I'm not sure there's anything I can do about it, but I'd like to ask your opinions."

They both smiled.

"Let's hear all about it," said TJ.

Reid almost regretted bringing it up. Almost. Some part of him wanted to talk about it, and that part wanted to find a way to see the redhead and Owen again. "When I was checking into the hotel this afternoon, I saw a woman. A very attractive woman. It was one of those moments I've heard people talk about; your eyes meet, you feel a connection ..." He shrugged. He'd always thought that kind of talk sounded ridiculous, and it seemed even more so when he was the one speaking.

"Don't look like that," said TJ. "That's what happened with us the first time I saw Dani."

Reid looked at them, and Dani smiled back at him. "It is. The next time we saw each other didn't go so well, but we got the hang of it eventually."

TJ took hold of her hand. "Yeah, I almost screwed it up. What about you, though? Did you talk to her?"

"I did. I saw her again a little while later. She was with her son, and he was upset." He looked at TJ. "The kind of upset I remember all too well."

TJ raised an eyebrow.

"I don't know what had set him off, but he was one unhappy little guy. I went over to them and gave him my iPod."

"Bach?" asked TJ.

It made Reid smile that his brother remembered. "Yep. It worked like a charm. When he was calm, I carried him out so they could get a taxi." He blew out a sigh. "And that was it."

"Aww! That was so sweet of you to help her out."

TJ rolled his eyes. "Dani likes sweet."

She laughed and slapped his arm. "Most women do." She looked back at Reid. "It's like I said earlier. Women want someone who can understand how they're feeling and help them out. You obviously understood what the boy needed, and, as his mother, whatever he needed, was what she needed. You didn't ask for her number or anything?"

He shook his head. "The cab driver was in a hurry. I didn't have the time or the foresight to plan my approach."

"So, she just rode away, and that's it?"

"It appears that way. I can't think of anything I can do that wouldn't seem totally creepy or stalkerish."

"And what can you think of that would seem that way?" asked Dani.

Reid gave her a sheepish smile. "I will admit that I've given some consideration to ways I could track her down. I believe she was at the hotel for a massage, or at least, an appointment at the spa. I could start there. Or I could somehow figure out which cab firm took her and where they dropped her."

TJ pursed his lips. "Sorry, Reid, but you're right, both those options seem kind of stalkerish to me."

Reid nodded. "That's the conclusion I reached, too. So, I suppose I have to file it away in my mind as a brief encounter, something that could have been—but wasn't."

"Aww." Dani looked so sad it was almost comical. "I don't want you to give up." She blew out a big sigh. "It could have been the beginning of something beautiful."

"Possibly. On the other hand, perhaps it's for the best."

TJ nodded. "Maybe so."

Dani looked from him to Reid and back again. "But it could have been something wonderful. She might have been your person."

Reid smiled. "Possibly, but now I'll never know."

"How can you be so fatalistic?"

He laughed. "I think it's called being realistic. In a city with a population of around four million people, I don't think my chances of running into her again are too great."

"I suppose not, and if you really wanted to see her again, you'd be more proactive, so I suppose I should just shut up. But when you said you wanted our opinions, I thought you were looking for suggestions."

"I wondered what you'd both say. I'm surprised at myself that I'm still thinking about it."

TJ nodded. "I am, too. I would have thought you'd have dismissed it by now. Are you sure you don't want to track her down—stalkerish or not?"

Reid thought about it. "I think the honest answer is that I do want to, but I'm not going to."

Dani nodded sadly. "Well, only you know what you want—but if you change your mind, let me know. I'd be happy to help."

"Thanks." Reid appreciated the offer and wasn't totally convinced that he wouldn't take her up on it.

~ ~ ~

Tara closed the apartment door behind her and made sure it was locked. The neighborhood wasn't bad, but she'd never felt totally safe living here. It was all she could afford, so it had to do, but she still wished she could move herself and Owen out of the city. Her dream was to move to Wyoming. She'd never been there, but it sounded so right. She was convinced it would be the perfect place for her and Owen.

"Are we going to Aunt Nicole's?" Owen asked as she took hold of his hand.

"No, not today. We're going to the park."

Owen nodded solemnly and trudged along beside her like a convicted man going to the gallows. The park wasn't his favorite place, but he tolerated it. Tara was convinced that the fresh air did him good. And, although he didn't really play with the other kids, she hoped that being around them did something for him.

Twenty minutes later, she sat on one of the benches, watching him. While the other kids ran and played, he sat on the edge of the playground, sorting the rocks and pebbles he found. She smiled to herself, knowing that in his own way, he was happy and enjoying himself.

"Hey, you." Carolann who lived in Tara's building plonked herself down on the bench beside her. "How's it going?"

"It's going. How about you?"

"About the same. The kids are driving me nuts, so I brought them out here to blow off some steam. You don't know how lucky you are with Owen. He's a doll; he's so quiet and well behaved."

Tara smiled. She did know how lucky she was—despite the way other people might see it. "He's a good kid, but so are your two. They all have their different personalities, just like we do."

Carolann smiled. "I guess. I mean, I couldn't live my life the way you do. You never go anywhere or do anything."

"Hey, I'll have you know I went for a massage yesterday, at a big fancy hotel in the city."

"Well, get you." Carolann laughed. "And other than that, when was the last time you went anywhere or did anything—and going to the grocery store doesn't count."

Tara laughed with her. "Okay. You got me. But you know how things are for me."

"I do, and I worry about you. You're like a recluse, only you live in the city instead of out in the mountains in the middle of nowhere."

"Hey. It's not that bad."

"I know. I just wish you'd join in more with the rest of us."

Tara shrugged. "I wish I could, but most of the time, it's not worth it."

"Well, how would you feel about coming with me and Deb tomorrow?"

"Where?"

"We're going to the community center over on Gascoigne street."

"Why?" Tara had heard of the place. Some of the single moms from her building hung out there sometimes, but she didn't think that was something she and Owen would enjoy.

"They're having a big book drive, collecting books for the kids and the vets. My two have so many books they've outgrown, I want to take them over there. It's nice to think that other kids might get to enjoy them. I think reading's important, and if you get into it when you're a kid, it's something that you have for a lifetime."

Tara smiled. She certainly felt that way. "What kind of books do they want?"

"Anything and everything they can get. Kids' books, adults' books. In the article I read about it, it said that the vets enjoy reading and it's a good escape for them. You know, it gets them out of their heads, so they don't keep reliving their own nightmares."

"I can see that. I love to escape into a good book when I can. In fact, I've probably got a whole bunch I could bring." She wasn't sure about taking Owen's books. He got so attached to his things and got upset when he couldn't find them, but she had shelves and shelves of books that she'd never read again. She wasn't thrilled at the prospect of giving them away, but she had them all on her e-reader anyway, and if the vets would enjoy them, it would be worth it.

"I don't know if the vets would want to read all those romances you work on."

Tara chuckled. "I doubt it, but I went through a phase of only reading mysteries and thrillers for a few years after my divorce—romance didn't interest me much at that point."

"Okay. I bet they'd enjoy those. So, are you going to come with us?"

"Yeah. Why not. As long as Owen's doing okay. What time are you going?"

"Deb's coming to my place for lunch, and then we'll leave around two. Do you want to have lunch with us?"

Tara shook her head. She knew Carolann would understand.

"Just give me a call ten minutes before you're ready to leave, and we'll meet you in the lobby."

Chapter Four

Reid looked around the lobby as he waited for Oscar to pick him up. He wasn't really seeing the other guests coming and going. He was seeing the redhead as he'd seen her yesterday—sitting by the concierge desk when he'd been checking in. Even thinking about that moment when their eyes first met sent a jolt through him. It didn't make any sense, but that no longer seemed to matter. It was undeniable that every time he thought about her, he had a physiological reaction. He'd spent far too much time last night reliving every moment of their brief encounter. He had so many questions—who was she? Was she even available? By the way she'd reacted to him, he believed she was interested in him—but that didn't necessarily mean that she wasn't married or involved with someone. Where was Owen's father? Did they return to him after she bid Reid such a wistful farewell? Had the wistfulness only been on his part? No. He knew that. If that damned cab driver hadn't been in such a hurry, there would have been more between them. He shook his head. There hadn't been anything more between them, no numbers exchanged—no means to ever contact her again. He needed to put her out of his mind, forget her, but he couldn't do it.

He got to his feet. Sitting here wishing he'd done differently wasn't going to change anything. He made his way out front to wait for Oscar. That would save some time—and maybe the doorman from yesterday would be out there.

He didn't get a chance to see if it was the same doorman or to decide if there was any point asking him about which cab companies they used. Oscar's limo pulled up at the same time as he walked out the doors.

The rear passenger window slid down, and Oscar grinned out at him. "Reid! Jump in."

Reid slid into the back, and Oscar punched his arm. "Always such perfect timing. It's like you planned it and Darren somehow fell in with your plan."

Reid smiled at Darren, the driver, in the rearview mirror. "We're on the same wavelength, right?"

Darren laughed. "I wish. I doubt my mind could ever turn itself up to the frequencies you operate on, but this worked out pretty well."

Reid smiled. "It did. Thanks for coming to get me."

"Hey. What about me?"

Reid laughed at Oscar. "You didn't come to get me, you made Darren drive since you're too lazy."

"I'm not lazy. I'm working damned hard these days—I work two jobs, keeping the club going and helping at the center."

"I never thought I'd see you running a community center, but I'm glad Grace got you involved. It's done you good."

Oscar smiled. "It has. She has. She's the best thing that's ever happened to me."

"I know, but you're kind of good for her too. It sounds like you're turning the center around, and this book drive is a fantastic idea."

"It is, but I can't take the credit for it. It's the brainchild of one of the vets, Daquan. I thought TJ would have told you about it—warned you that Daquan is one of your biggest fans and might get a little tongue-tied."

"No. He didn't talk about it at all. To be fair, neither did you. I only heard about it from Mom."

Oscar shrugged. "You tend to stay busy up there in Washington doing your own thing."

"I do, but books are my thing—you don't think mine are good enough?"

"What do you mean?"

"I mean you're doing a book drive and you didn't think to mention it to your brother who happens to be a writer."

"Oh. Sorry. I didn't even make the connection."

Reid laughed. "You're not much of a reader, are you?"

"No. Grace is the reader. She loves your books."

"She read them?"

"She did."

Reid smiled. "So, both my sisters-in-law read them, but neither of my brothers did."

Oscar chuckled. "If you were anyone else I'd worry that it hurt your feelings somehow, but you don't have feelings."

Reid rolled his eyes. "I do; I just don't feel them the same way you do."

Oscar frowned. "You're not offended, are you? That I didn't tell you about the book drive or try to involve you?"

"Relax. Of course, I'm not offended. I was just surprised that you missed such a logical connection. But you aren't always efficient, I know that. So, I took things into my own hands and came down here. I've had some of my books sent down. I have a check for Grace to buy whatever new books she thinks are best—for the kids and the vets. And I have another idea, but I wanted to run it by you—and her and TJ and whoever else needs a say."

"What idea?"

"Where do you plan to house all these books?"

Oscar shrugged. "At the center."

"Do you have the space?"

"I thought so at first, but this whole thing got bigger than we expected, faster than we expected."

Reid nodded. "That's what I expected."

Oscar chuckled. "Of course, it is. So, what's your solution?"

"A bus. A book bus. Like a mobile library. It'd serve double duty as storage and a library. It's a safe place to keep the books and for people to go to read. I believe this may grow to be much bigger than you thought, and you could end up with a fleet of buses that can go out into the communities."

Oscar raised an eyebrow. "You could be right. You need to talk to Grace and Daquan. I try to mostly just do as I'm told at the center. Grace and TJ take the lead—and like I said, this whole thing was Daquan's idea, so he should get some input."

Reid nodded. "It is only an idea. I don't mean to come in and try to take anything over. I just got enthusiastic when I heard about it."

Oscar grinned. "I'm happy you did. Seems like the center is becoming a real family affair. Maybe we can get you to move down here and join us."

Reid shook his head rapidly. "No. I'll buy you a bus, but I couldn't live here. You know that."

"I do. I was just getting carried away with enthusiasm myself. I like the idea of the three of us getting closer again. Now we need to find you a woman, and if nothing else, we can all meet up in Montana for weekends and get-togethers."

Reid nodded. He could see that happening. He even liked the idea. Oscar and TJ were both spending more time back in Montana lately. He'd been back for Oscar and Grace's engagement party and planned to go again soon. Maybe he'd go and catch up with Shane, as TJ had suggested.

"Did I fuck up talking about finding you a woman?"

Reid laughed. "No. Obviously, I don't have one, but ..."

"But?"

"The idea doesn't horrify me as much as it used to."

Oscar brought his hand up to his face.

"You never did manage to hide your smile when you do that, you know?"

Oscar moved his thumb over his lips. "I know. It worked when I was a kid, and somehow I've never broken the habit."

"What are you smiling about anyway?"

"The fact that you aren't totally averse to the possibility of meeting someone."

Reid held his gaze. He almost told him about the redhead yesterday, but he stopped himself. There was no point.

~ ~ ~

Owen sat on Tara's lap on the bus and stared out the window. She wondered, as she did so often, what was going on inside that little head of his. He watched the traffic and people on the sidewalk with a frown furrowing his little brow as if he were trying to figure them out the same way he did with his puzzle pieces.

Deb turned in her seat to look back at them. "How have you been? I'm glad you came with us, I haven't seen you in ages."

"I've been busy. I just finished editing a book on Tuesday, and I'm not starting another until Monday, so I have a couple of days to relax."

"That's good. I worry about you, cooped up in your apartment all the time with Owen." She waggled her fingers at him and smiled, trying to get a reaction, but Owen's gaze didn't flicker away from the window.

Deb made a face. "He doesn't like me."

"I've told you a thousand times. It's nothing personal. It's not that he doesn't like you; it's just that he doesn't really notice you. You don't capture his attention."

Deb laughed. "Story of my life! Cute guys never notice me."

Carolann leaned across the aisle. "That's not true. That guy last Saturday was cute, and he more than noticed you—all night long, I believe."

Deb laughed. "He was cute. The kids were staying with Mom, so why not?"

Tara smiled. It was fun to hear about the girls' antics on their nights out. It seemed Deb managed to find a guy to go home with most weekends. Tara was grateful that she had a built-in excuse not to join them. They didn't even ask anymore. She'd never been the type to go out drinking and partying and going home with random men.

"I can never tell with you," said Deb. "The way you smile like that when we talk about girls' night. I can't figure out if you're trying to hide your disapproval, or if you're jealous that you're not getting any."

Tara laughed. "Neither. I don't disapprove. It's fun to hear about, but even if I could go with you, I wouldn't want to. It's not my thing."

Carolann grinned at her. "You don't need a real guy to get off with. You get off on those dirty books you edit, don't you? Go on, admit it!"

Tara laughed. "Okay, I admit it. I do get involved in the characters' lives—and most of them have rather interesting sex lives." She glanced down at Owen, but he was still staring intently out the window.

"I need to read some of them," said Deb. "It seems to me that getting my sex from a book would be a lot less hassle than a real man. They're more trouble than they're worth."

Tara nodded. For some reason, mystery man's face popped into her mind. She'd rather get her sex from him as Deb put it than read about it in a book. But, that wasn't an option. She'd missed her chance.

They all got up and gathered their bags as the bus approached the stop near the center. Owen clung tightly to her hand as they got off. She looked down at him, he was stressed, she could tell. He was used to riding on the bus, but now they were in an unfamiliar place—and about to enter an unfamiliar environment. She smiled at him. "Are you okay?"

He nodded uncertainly.

"What do you need?"

"Music."

She smiled. She hadn't been able to get the iPod off him until after he'd fallen asleep last night. This morning they'd been too busy going through his usual routines and getting books together to bring. Fortunately, she'd popped the iPod into her purse just before they left the apartment. She fished it out, and his little face lit up when he saw it. She didn't see any reason not to let him listen to it while they went into the center to deliver the books.

Carolann and Deb were a long way ahead of them already. They stopped and looked back to see if she was coming. She waved them to go on. "We'll catch up with you inside." She'd already told them not to worry about her and Owen riding the bus home with them. She needed to be free to stay for as long or as short a time as Owen could handle.

Owen was already putting the earbuds in his ears. She handed him the iPod, and he pressed the buttons, fast forwarding—searching for something, apparently.

"What are you looking for?"

He didn't answer until he'd forwarded a few more times, then he looked up at her with a smile that filled her heart with happiness. "Bach."

She took his hand and picked up the heavy book bag. She still had more books she wanted to donate, but there was no way she could have carried them all. It'd take another two trips at least. She was hoping that they'd maybe have a collection point somewhere closer to her apartment.

She stopped outside the center. There was an elderly guy sitting outside the main door in a wheelchair. She looked down at Owen, but he was lost in his own world, listening to the music.

"Good morning, Miss." The old guy smiled warmly, and Tara smiled back. "Are you coming in?"

"We are. I have some books to deliver."

"That's very kind of you. Come on in." He smiled at Owen. "Are you getting rid of your books, so you can get some new ones?" he asked.

The little furrows appeared on Owen's brow, but he didn't reply. He just stared.

The old man didn't seem perturbed. He smiled up at her. "Shy, is he?"

She nodded. That was the simplest explanation.

"He'll be fine. There's a whole bunch of kiddies in there today. He'll be joining in and playing with the rest of 'em in no time."

"No, we're only here to drop off the books."

The old man looked up into her eyes. His were a steely blue, and they made her feel he could see into her soul. "Are you okay? Is he?"

She nodded and tried to smile reassuringly. "We are. It's just that Owen isn't like the other kids. We tend to keep to ourselves—it's easier that way. We only came to deliver the books."

He nodded. "It might be easier that way, but it isn't always better. You should come down here sometimes. Hang out with us if you need some company—both of you."

Tara smiled. She liked him; crazy as it seemed, she felt more at home with him than she did with the two girls she'd come with. "Thanks."

He nodded. "I can see you don't plan to take me up on the offer, but think about it. If ever you need a place or people who understand, you know where we are."

"Thanks." She didn't know what else to say, and she was in danger of spilling her guts to the old guy, telling him how tough things were, how lonely she felt, and how afraid of the future she was—for Owen's sake and her own. He reached up and gave her hand a squeeze. "You can do it, girl, but you don't have to do it all by yourself if you don't want."

A tear escaped and rolled down her cheek, taking her by surprise. "Thank you."

"What? For making you cry?" He smiled. "I didn't mean to do that. Why don't you take them books inside? I'm Terry, by the way." He held his hand out, and she shook with him.

"I'm Tara, and this is Owen."

"Well, thanks for coming to see us, Miss Tara. I hope I'll see you again." He smiled at Owen, and to Tara's surprise, Owen smiled back at him.

She heaved the strap of the bag higher on her shoulder and went inside. She'd be glad to get rid of them at this point—they were heavy.

Chapter Five

Reid stood inside Grace's office, looking out the window. From here he could observe the crowded center without having to be in the middle of it all. There must be several dozen people out there, at least. Oscar, Grace, and TJ had all introduced him to people—to vets and youngsters, and old ladies. They were all regulars at the center. Most of the people out there at the moment were just visiting—coming to drop off books. He smiled at that. He didn't tend to have much faith in humans, finding them to be self-serving mostly and generally oblivious to others' needs. It pleased him to see that when a need was pointed out to them, they were coming out to help—even though he believed that it was still self-serving. They wanted to donate their old books so that they could feel good about themselves for being charitable. He turned away from the window, realizing that wasn't a very charitable thought.

Grace smiled at him. "I really should get out there to show my face and thank people. These Friday afternoon open house sessions have been really good. But I have to be realistic about it. The initial interest in the book drive was driven by an article Dani wrote for us. People are good to come and donate, but I know at least some of it is driven by interest in seeing Oscar Davenport and his fiancée."

Reid smiled. "You don't mind that?"

She made a face. "I wouldn't choose it, but it's my reality, so I'm not above using it to my advantage."

"We're more alike than I would have imagined."

Grace chuckled. "We are. We come from different places, but it has the same outcome."

He cocked his head to one side.

"You aren't big on emotions; you don't see the point in them unless they serve some useful purpose. I grew up not having the luxury of emotions being a factor. Just because something made me sad, uncomfortable, or afraid, it didn't mean I could do anything about it. I learned to observe emotions, and since I couldn't indulge in them, I at least learned to capitalize on them."

Reid nodded. "That almost makes you sound cold and calculating though, and I know that you're not."

She smiled. "Another benefit is that I don't care how I might seem—unless I can use it to my advantage. I know who I am; I know my intentions; the people who matter do, too."

Reid chuckled. "You're a smart lady, Grace."

"Thanks, that's a huge compliment coming from you. Now, do you want to come out there with me—or would you rather hide out in here?"

"I'll come out there. I'd like to talk to Daquan."

She laughed. "Just go easy on him? I think he might be a little tongue-tied around you."

Reid smiled. "We should do fine together, then."

Grace opened the door. "I think he's in the kitchen. Do you want me to find him for you?"

"That's okay. You do your thing. I can find him." He watched Grace greet people and stop and chat. She was good at this. A natural. He drew in a deep breath. He, on the other hand, was anything but a natural with people. He'd rather avoid them; he wouldn't have chosen today to come to the center if he'd known it was an open house like this for book donations.

He started to make his way to the kitchen, hoping he'd find Daquan there and be able to have a quiet conversation. He skirted the long line of people holding bags and boxes of books they were waiting to hand over. There were all kinds of people—young and old and apparently rich and poor, too. He stopped and did a double take when he spotted a small boy in the line. A small boy with a rapturous smile on his face as he swung his head as if to music.

His heart began to thunder in his chest. It was Owen! And he was listening to music—he had Reid's iPod clutched tightly in his little hand. His other hand was holding tight to his mom's. It was her. The redhead with the big blue eyes and the long, long legs. He closed his eyes for a moment, half expecting that when he opened them again, she and Owen would be gone. They weren't. They were still there—except now she was staring at him, and Owen was tugging on her hand. He let go of her and ran across the crowded room toward Reid with a big smile on his face.

Reid squatted down to greet him. He wanted to hug the kid but knew better. So, it came as a huge surprise when Owen flung his arms around his neck and leaned his cheek against Reid's for a brief moment. Then he stepped back and smiled. "Music," he said happily as if that explained everything.

Reid smiled back at him. "Music," he agreed. "You like the music?"

Owen nodded happily.

"Owen!"

They both looked up to see his mom staring down at them. "Don't run off like that."

"I'm sorry." Reid felt responsible.

She looked into his eyes, and there it was again, that feeling, that connection. "It is you."

He got to his feet. "It is." He couldn't think what else to say. The nearness of her threw him. She was even more beautiful up close. She smelled good. She was a few inches shorter than him … and noting those facts wasn't the best use of his time now he'd found her again! He smiled, and she smiled back. He had to pull himself together. He couldn't let her walk away again. He held out his hand. "I'm Reid. I didn't even ask your name yesterday."

She smiled and shook with him. The feel of her hand in his sent a current rushing through him. It took him all the way back to his childhood. Echoes of Shane's voice rang in his head. The first time you ever touch a girl, watch her face, don't worry about what she says, watch her face, especially her eyes, that's how you can tell if she really likes you.

If that were true, then she did like him. Her pupils dilated, a touch of color flushed her cheeks. "I'm Tara."

"I'm Owen, I'm Owen!"

Reid dragged his gaze away from Tara's to look down at the kid. "I know. It's good to see you again, Owen."

Owen smiled up at him.

"It's good to see you again, too."

Reid looked back up Tara. Had he imagined that? No, judging by the now deep flush on her cheeks, she'd really said it. "It's good to see you, too. I feared I never would."

She nodded. "I didn't think we'd be able to get your iPod back to you."

He smiled. "It was a gift."

"Thank you. I think it might be his favorite gift ever."

"I'm glad." Reid was still smiling at her, and she was still smiling back. The color was slowly fading from her cheeks. Her embarrassment might be receding, but this would get awkward quickly if he didn't pull himself together, figure out what to say next. He looked at the heavy bag she had over her shoulder. "Are you here to donate books?"

"Yes. I read a lot, but now I have all my books on my e-reader. I heard what they were doing here and wanted to share the escapes that I've enjoyed. Are you doing the same?"

"No." He almost wished he'd said yes. "I … err … my brother and his fiancée run the place. They're behind the book drive. I'm just here to …err … help out."

She nodded, though now she wasn't smiling.

"Do you want me to take the bag for you?"

"I'm fine, thanks. I should get back in the line."

"Can I join you?"

Owen made the decision for them. He took hold of Reid's hand and smiled up at his mom. "Books."

Tara drew in a deep breath. She could hardly tell Owen no, that he should leave the nice man alone. She didn't want to tell him no. She just didn't want mystery man to feel obliged to hang out with them. Reid. He was no longer a mystery man—unfortunately. His explanation that he was here to help his brother had made clear who he was. He was a Davenport.

Oscar Davenport and his fiancée had been all over the local news with the good work they were doing here. There was a second brother—TJ, a vet who had also gotten involved, and there had been some speculation in the article she'd read about whether the third brother would make an appearance. And now he had. He was walking beside her, holding Owen's hand—which was a minor miracle in itself.

When they reached the end of the line, she stopped and turned to smile at him. "Thanks again for letting him keep the iPod. It's very kind of you."

Reid smiled. He had an amazing smile. "It's my pleasure. I'm glad it helped him."

"You were a lifesaver yesterday. He loves it. I did some research last night. I had no idea about classical music and brain frequencies."

Reid smiled. "Most people don't. There's been quite a lot of research done, but it's not something most people ever need to know."

"Well, thanks to you, I know about it now—and it really does help him. He's so much calmer and happier."

"I'm glad it can help him—and I hope that helps you."

"It does. You have no idea. He's a good boy, but it's hard."

He nodded. "I can imagine."

They took a couple of steps forward as the line advanced. Tara wanted to ask him how he'd known what Owen's problem was yesterday—how he'd understood that the music would help. He'd said he didn't have an autistic child—or any children, thank goodness. That reminded her. She surreptitiously peeked at his left hand. No ring. Yay! Then she felt stupid. What did it matter?

He met her gaze as she looked back up. "You felt it, too, yesterday, didn't you?"

She wanted to ask what he meant, but she didn't need to. She nodded.

"I thought I'd blown my chance to get to know you. Now I've been given a second chance. What do you think?"

This time she did ask the stalling question—but only because she didn't want to make a fool of herself. "About what?"

"Would you like to get to know each other?"

Her heart hammered in her chest. Of course, she'd love to. But what did he mean? She knew Oscar Davenport's reputation; he was that guy who slept with every woman who crossed his path. Was Reid the same? Was he asking if she wanted to sleep with him? Hell, yes, she'd love to, but hell, no, she wasn't that kind of girl. "How?" was the only way she could phrase the question without making a fool of herself.

He shrugged. "I thought maybe we could start with dinner?"

She shook her head sadly, realizing that it didn't matter what he meant. She couldn't go for dinner with him any more than she'd jump into bed with him—she couldn't leave Owen.

His green eyes bore into hers. "You don't want to?"

She sighed. "I'd love to, but it just isn't possible. I have Owen." She smiled down at the little guy who was still holding onto Reid's hand and moving his head to the music.

"I had noticed. I think he's okay with me."

She smiled. "You have no idea how much more than okay with you he is. He won't hold anyone's hand—not even my sister's. I couldn't believe that he let you carry him out yesterday, and today when he ran to you, I was speechless."

"I was kind of pleased myself. So, since I like Owen and he likes me … Why can't you go for dinner with me?"

"Because I can't leave him."

Reid reached up and straightened the collar of his polo shirt. "You don't have anyone to babysit?"

"It's not that. I can't leave him with anyone. He doesn't do well. When you saw us yesterday? That was the first time I'd left him in months. He stayed with my sister while I went to the hotel for a massage. He got upset. She had to bring him to me."

Reid nodded slowly. "I see."

Her heart sank. He was going to accept her explanation and that would be an end to it. She wondered how long he'd continue to even stand in line with them.

He smiled. "Where is he comfortable?"

"What do you mean?"

"Well, I can hardly invite myself over to your place. I could ask you to come to my place, but my place is a room at the hotel—and I'm guessing he won't be very comfortable there after yesterday. Even apart from the fact that you shouldn't accept an invite to a stranger's hotel room when you don't know that I'm not a serial killer." He sounded serious, but the corners of his lips curved up in a small smile as he spoke. "So, is there someplace he likes to go to eat? Or a park where we could take a picnic?"

She stared at him for a long moment. She'd expected him to accept her refusal, and here he was trying to come up with ways to make it happen anyway.

His smile faded. "Or did I miss the point? Was Owen just an excuse to give me the brush off?"

"No! I'd love to go to dinner with you, to get to know you. I just …" Her mind was racing. How could she make it work? "You can't exactly invite yourself over to my place, but I can invite you. I'd love to have you over, and we both know Owen would."

He was even more handsome when he smiled. "In that case, thank you. But let me bring dinner?"

She laughed. "If I didn't know better I'd think you'd already heard how terrible my cooking is!"

He laughed with her. "No, but that information has now been logged for future reference."

That made her smile. She'd love to hope that he might need to refer to that information in the future, but she doubted it. Snippets of information about the third Davenport brother were trickling back into her mind. He didn't live in LA. He lived in Washington state.

"How about I bring whatever your favorite takeout is?"

She wanted to pinch herself. She must be dreaming. Mystery man was coming to dinner; he was good with Owen, and now he wanted to bring her favorite so that she didn't have to cook.

"I'm a woman of simple tastes."

He smiled. "So, what am I bringing?"

"Veggie pizza. Of course, that means you can bring whatever you like, too."

"A large veggie pizza it is, then."

"There you are." They both looked up as a guy put his hand on Reid's shoulder. "I was wondering where—"

They all looked down as Owen screamed. He tugged on Reid's hand, trying to get him away from the newcomer. Tara bent down to him, but Reid beat her to it. He scooped Owen up and rested his forehead against his. To her amazement, Owen stopped screaming and focused intently on looking into Reid's eyes.

"It's okay, Owen." Reid spoke in a slow monotone. "That's TJ. He's my brother."

Owen slid a sideways glance at TJ and then looked back into Reid's eyes. "He hurt you."

Tara felt tears sting her eyes. She couldn't believe that Owen was already so attached to Reid that he wanted to protect him. "No. He doesn't want to hurt me. He loves me. I love him." He reached his arm out, and TJ stepped closer. Reid slung his arm around his shoulders and smiled. "See? He's good."

Owen sat back and eyed TJ suspiciously for a long few moments. Then he smiled. "Good."

"This is Owen," Reid told TJ.

Owen wriggled, and when Reid set him down, he took up the same position he'd had before—by Reid's side, holding his hand.

TJ smiled at him, and he smiled back. "Good."

"Sorry about that," TJ looked up at them.

"Please don't apologize," said Tara. "You couldn't know."

"It's fine," said Reid. "You just startled him."

"And this is Owen? From yesterday?"

Tara looked at him and then at Reid.

"Yes. From yesterday." He smiled at her. "I told him about meeting you."

"You did?" Tara was stunned. She'd believed that he'd probably forgotten all about her the moment the cab door closed.

He nodded. "And sorry, Tara, this is my brother, TJ. TJ, this is Tara."

TJ smiled at her. "So, we know your name now."

"We do."

"And you just happened to be here donating books today and ran into this guy again?"

"I couldn't believe it when I saw him—well, it was Owen who spotted him."

"Quite a coincidence, huh?" Tara got the impression that TJ didn't believe it was a coincidence, but there was nothing she could say to convince him otherwise. She couldn't even blame him. Now she knew that they were the Davenports, she could understand it; they probably had women stalking them all the time.

Reid gave his brother a warning look. She wanted to reassure them both, but she knew she'd only make it worse if she tried.

She was relieved to see the old guy in the wheelchair coming toward them wearing a big grin. "Miss Tara. You're still here?" He noticed the way Owen was still clinging to Reid's hand. "I didn't realize you guys know each other. What's the story?"

Tara looked at Reid. She didn't know how to answer, and it seemed he didn't either. He laughed. "We haven't written it yet, Terry."

Chapter Six

"Are you coming over for dinner tonight?" Grace asked Reid. The center was much quieter now, and they were all sitting in Grace's office.

TJ frowned. "You haven't told them?"

Reid shook his head. He already knew that TJ was suspicious of Tara. He could understand why, randomly running into each other two days in row seemed a bit of a stretch, but Reid knew that far-fetched as it seemed, it really was coincidence—a very happy coincidence, as far as he was concerned.

"Told us what?" asked Dani.

"That the woman he ran into at the hotel yesterday just happened to show up here today and invited him to dinner tonight." TJ was still frowning.

"She was here?" Dani looked delighted.

Reid smiled at her, glad that she shared his enthusiasm. "I couldn't believe my luck."

"I can't believe it's just luck either," said TJ.

"Somebody fill me in," said Oscar.

"He met a woman in the hotel lobby yesterday. Then she just shows up here today," said TJ. "I don't like it."

"You're just too suspicious," said Dani. "I think it's amazing."

Oscar gave Reid an inquiring look.

"I understand where TJ's coming from. It does seem like too much of a coincidence. But she was as surprised to see me again as I was to see her."

"What happened yesterday?" asked Grace.

"Nothing really. I saw her when I was checking in. Just noticed an attractive woman. Then I saw her again a little later, and her son was upset. I talked to them, gave the little boy my iPod because I knew the music would help calm him. Then I put them in a taxi, and they left."

"You didn't get her number?" asked Oscar.

"No, but as soon as she'd gone, I wished I had."

Grace looked thoughtful. "I'm with TJ. I find it a bit suspicious."

"I don't," said Oscar. "I think it's awesome."

Dani grinned. "I think it's like fate. It was meant to be."

Reid chuckled. "I don't know about that."

"And you're going for dinner with her?" asked Grace.

He nodded.

"Tell them where," said TJ.

"I'm going to her place."

Grace frowned. "I don't like that. Why there? Why not go out somewhere? It's not just women who are safer in a public place. It could be some kind of set up."

Reid shook his head. "It's not. I know it isn't. It was my suggestion."

Grace and TJ exchanged a look.

"Come on, guys. I'm not stupid. Owen, her little boy, is autistic. She doesn't go anywhere without him. I thought he'd be more comfortable if I went there."

Oscar blew out a sigh. "I'm liking this less."

Reid raised an eyebrow at him.

"I don't think it's a setup or anything, but what's the point?"

Grace scowled at him, and Oscar laughed. "All I'm saying is

that you're only here for a week. Why not go out with someone who can actually go out? Find someone you can take to dinner, have fun with."

Reid shook his head. "Because I don't want to. There's something about her. I want to get to know her, and the way to do that is to go to her place. I don't know why it's such a big deal. I didn't try to have any input about the way you guys all got to know each other. I appreciate that you care, but this is my business."

TJ nodded. "You're right. It is. Go. I hope you have fun, but I'm going to need her address and phone number."

Dani laughed. "You sound as though he's going to be abducted while he's there or something."

TJ nodded. "And if he is, we'll at least have a starting point."

They all laughed, but Reid knew that TJ wasn't joking. This was hard for him. "Okay. I'll give you her address and her number if that will make you feel better."

"It will."

"What time are you going?" asked Dani.

"I said I'd be there at seven."

Oscar checked his watch. "Do you want Darren to take you back to the hotel, then?"

"That'd be great. Thanks."

~ ~ ~

Tara paced around the kitchen. Was she crazy? She'd never invited a man to her apartment before. It wasn't what a single woman should do. She knew that. Then again, it was something Deb and Carolann did all the time. They went out, got drunk and took guys home with them. They were still alive! And they invited guys from the club. She'd only gone and invited Reid Davenport! She'd googled him when she and

Owen got home. He was a programmer, who'd developed some apps. He was also a writer! She shook her head and blew out a sigh. She didn't really have to worry about him being a serial killer, she was fairly sure of that. She probably wouldn't have to worry about anything other than tonight. He lived in Washington state—the San Juan Islands, no less. She didn't know how long he'd be in LA, but she doubted it'd be more than a few days. Her biggest worry should be about Owen. He'd taken such a shine to Reid already. The last thing he needed was to get attached to someone he'd probably never see again.

Her phone rang, and she jumped. Maybe it was him? Perhaps he'd changed his mind and wasn't coming after all.

"Hello?"

"Hey. You didn't call me."

"Oh, hey, Nic. Sorry. We went out this afternoon."

"Oh, good. Where did you go?"

"We went to the community center over on Gascoigne Street with Carolann and Deb. They're having a book drive, and I wanted to give some of my old books."

"Cool. I'm glad you got out. How's Owen today?"

"He's great."

"Still listening to mystery man's music?"

Tara had to smile. "He is. And you're not going to believe this, but we ran into him again today, at the center."

"Mystery man? Seriously? Is he stalking you or something?"

Tara laughed. "No. He's not. His brother thinks I'm stalking him."

"His brother?"

Tara drew in a deep breath, not sure how her sister would react. "Yeah, it turns out that my mystery man is actually Reid Davenport. His brothers TJ and Oscar Davenport run the center. That's why he was there."

"Reid Davenport? Holy shit, Tara!"

She laughed. "Yeah, that's what I thought when I realized who he was."

"Damn, girl. Tell me you got his number this time?"

"I did, and he got mine, too. In fact, he's coming over for dinner tonight."

"Coming over?"

"Yeah. He asked me to go out for dinner, but I couldn't—because of Owen."

"Do you think that's a good idea?"

"Yeah, I don't see why not. Owen likes him. It'll be easier here than trying to keep Owen happy if we went out someplace."

"I don't mean is it good for Owen, I mean is it safe for you?"

"It is. He's a good man. You can just tell."

"He'd better be. Are you sure he is who you think is?"

"I am. I looked him up online, and there are photos of him and everything. It really is him."

"Okay, then. But it makes me nervous."

Tara laughed. "I'm nervous, too. Though I shouldn't be. It's just dinner. He's only here visiting his brothers. It's no big deal."

"No big deal? You're dating a Davenport, and you say it's no big deal?"

"I'm not dating him, we're just having dinner, that's all. I'm sure he'll leave in a few days, and that will be the end of it. You're the one who encouraged me that I should have a life, even if it's only for a few hours here and there. So, this evening, for a few hours, I will have a life. I'll have a kind, handsome guy, who Owen likes a lot, over for dinner. Then he'll be gone and I'll go back to my normal—and you'll be nagging me that I should do more."

"I suppose. But be careful. I wish he wasn't going to your place."

"It'll be fine. Don't worry."

"Of course, I'm going to worry. You have to call me when he leaves—no matter how late it is, okay?"

Tara laughed. "Okay, I'll call and let you know I'm still alive."

"It's not funny. If he chops you up into little pieces, I'll never talk to you again."

"He won't. I promise. He's a good guy."

"Okay. But you'd better be right."

"I am. I'm going to go now. I want to give Owen a bath, and I need to get changed."

"What are you going to wear?"

"I have no idea. I don't know what one wears on a first date anymore, I haven't had one in years."

"Well, don't ask me. I never had a first date that I didn't go out on."

"It'll be fine, don't worry about me."

"I will. I'm sure it'll be okay, but it makes me nervous."

"I'll call you when he leaves. I promise."

After they'd hung up, Tara went to check on Owen. He was playing with his volcano. He loved that thing almost as much as he loved his dinosaurs. He looked up when he saw her standing there. "Play?" he asked.

She nodded and went to sit on the floor beside him. She hoped she wasn't being stupid letting Reid come over for dinner. If Owen didn't like him so much, there was no way she'd have agreed to it. Perhaps the fact that Owen liked him was a reason she should have said no. Either way, she had agreed to it, and she didn't want to back out now. It was just one evening—possibly an enjoyable break from their usual routine—possibly an unmitigated disaster, but whichever it turned out to be, it was only one evening. It was a risk worth taking.

~ ~ ~

"You don't have to wait," Reid told Darren when he brought the limo to a stop in front of Tara's apartment building. Darren smiled at him in the rearview mirror. "That's what you think. I'm under strict instructions from both your brothers and Grace, that I am not allowed to leave here without you. You stay as late as you like. All night if it works out that way, but I'll be sitting right here the whole time. I would, even if no one had told me to. I have to say, I'm not entirely comfortable with this setup."

Reid laughed. "She's a single mom, not some Mata Hari who's going to drug me and kidnap me."

Darren laughed with him. "I'm sure you're right, but can you imagine how we'd all feel if this chick really was a stalker and something happened to you?"

"Yeah, I suppose you have a point, but she isn't, I assure you."

"Okay, well, you'd better get going before your pizza gets cold. And like I said, stay as late as you want. Don't worry about me."

"Thanks, Darren." Reid got out and looked up at the building. It wasn't the most inviting looking place. But Tara and Owen were inside there somewhere, so he set out with his pizza toward the main doors.

The building was run down, but not dirty. The elevator smelled stale, and he held his breath until the doors opened on the twelfth floor. The hallway didn't smell much better. He followed the numbered doorways until he found 1222. That was her. He tried the doorbell but didn't hear any sound. He waited, not knowing if it was broken. Just when he was about to knock, the door opened, and there she was, smiling at him. She took his breath away. "Pizza delivery," he said with a smile.

"Great. Come on in." She stepped aside and gestured for him to go ahead of her.

For a moment, he hesitated. TJ and Grace's warnings filled his head. What if they were right? What if there was a guy waiting in the next room, ready to bash him on the head and knock him out? He stepped through into the living room. There was a guy there waiting for him, but the guy was about two and a half feet tall, and he didn't bash him on the head and knock him out; instead, he smiled up at him and tugged on his hand. "Volcano."

Reid smiled at him. "Volcano?"

Owen nodded eagerly. "Volcano."

Tara appeared beside him. "No, Owen. I told you, when Reid came we're going to eat pizza."

Owen frowned, and Reid hoped he wasn't going to get upset. Thankfully, he didn't. "No volcano?" he asked sadly.

"You can play for a few more minutes if you like," said Tara.

Reid watched him go.

"Do you want me to take that?" she asked.

He handed her the pizza box and followed her to the kitchen area. The apartment wasn't big. There was a sectional and a TV on one side, a kitchen that wasn't much more than a kitchenette on the other, and a small dining table. Owen had disappeared through one of three doors off the hallway into what Reid assumed must be his bedroom, with the others leading to a bathroom and Tara's room.

"What would you like to drink?"

"What are my options?"

"Beer, red wine, soda or water."

"I'll take a beer, please." It seemed safer than unidentified red wine.

She took two bottles from the fridge and handed one to him. "Are you ready to eat?"

He nodded. "We probably should. I don't think I got here as fast as a delivery driver would have."

She smiled. "I never invited a delivery driver inside before."

He smiled back. "I'm glad to hear it; that could be risky."

She laughed. "I think my sister believes this is even riskier."

He laughed with her. "She wasn't impressed?"

Tara shook her head. "Not one bit."

"If it's any consolation, my brother wasn't, either. Though what he thinks you might do to me, I don't know."

She smiled. "I could tell he thought I was stalking you this afternoon."

"It's nothing personal."

"No, I can understand his concern."

Reid raised an eyebrow.

"Well, I'm sure your family has to be careful."

"You know the name Davenport then?"

"I do."

He shrugged. He'd hoped she didn't. But the way she'd reacted at the center this afternoon when he'd told her that his brother ran the place had made it seem that she did. At least, she'd seemed uncomfortable about it—not eager to date a rich guy like so many other women. The silence lengthened as they stared at each other. It wasn't awkward. It felt comfortable— familiar—as if the two of them were connected by an understanding. Their siblings might be wary of the underlying motives behind this date, but the two of them knew. What did he know about her? He knew that she had a good heart. He had a feeling that, just as Dani had said, she was his person and he was hers. It wasn't a concept to which he'd ever given any credence until yesterday afternoon when he'd met her. But now it seemed like some irrefutable natural law. She was meant for him, and he was meant for her. Now all that remained was the not so minor detail of turning the concept into reality.

Eventually, she tore her gaze away from his. "I should ..." She picked up the pizza box and rummaged in a drawer to find the cutter.

Chapter Seven

Once they were all seated at the table, Reid raised his glass to her. "Here's to …" He hesitated, and she wondered what he was going to say. To us hardly seemed likely. To a pleasant evening, seemed the only reasonable thing to say, maybe to getting to know each other?

They both laughed as Owen filled the silence. "Bach," he said with a smile.

Reid nodded. "I like it. Here's to Bach, without whose music, we wouldn't be sitting here right now.

"To Bach." Tara was happy to toast her gratitude to the composer. She had a lot to be grateful to him for. He'd brought Reid into her life, even if it was just for this evening, and more than that, he seemed to be bringing her son much more peace than he'd known until now.

She smiled at Reid. "So, how long are you in the city for?" She might as well as know from the beginning.

"Just the week. I wanted to come and visit my brothers and see how the book drive was going."

She nodded. It was longer than she'd expected.

"How about you? Have you always lived here?"

"Yes, I grew up here. I always thought I'd move away someday, but it never worked out."

"Where would you go?"

She smiled. "You'll probably think I'm nuts, but I've been thinking about moving to Wyoming. Well, dreaming is probably a better word. I doubt I'll be able to make it happen."

"Why Wyoming?"

"Because I'd love for us to live somewhere like that. Somewhere quiet, rural, about as different from the city as you can get."

"It's definitely that. What do you do? Could you get a job in Wyoming?"

"I work from home." She smiled. "I'm a freelance editor."

He raised an eyebrow.

"Yes, Rupert, I know you write."

He chuckled. "Now I'm nervous; I feel like you'll be silently correcting my grammar."

She laughed. "No, you have no worries there. I'm an editor by trade, not by nature. I've only been doing it for the last few years. I enjoy it, but I still think of myself as a teacher."

"What kind of teacher?"

"A fourth-grade teacher. I loved it, but I couldn't find a way to keep doing it."

Reid cocked his head to one side. She liked the way he did that. He looked like a puppy who was trying to figure out her reasoning but couldn't.

"It's hard with Owen."

He nodded. "I imagine it is. You don't go anywhere without him?"

"No. Very rarely. Anyway, what about you?"

"What about me?"

"Well, I know you write, and I know you've developed some apps. What does your everyday look like?" She imagined it was very different from hers.

He smiled. "I work from home, too. I arrange my time in sections. For two months, I write and then the next two months I code. I find my brain works better with a break in between."

"You sound like Owen."

"That's probably because I am like Owen."

She put her fork down and stared at him. "That's how you knew about the music—that it would help?"

"Yep. I used to be very much like him at his age. As I've gotten older, I've found ways to cope."

"Wow! You have no idea how much hope that gives me."

He smiled. "I'm glad it does. I know when I was small, my folks thought I'd be that way for life. You should talk to my mom; she'd be better able to tell you how it was for her."

Tara shook her head. This evening seemed almost surreal. It was hard to believe that he was sitting here in her apartment having dinner—it was crazy enough that any guy should be sitting here doing that, especially when she'd only met him yesterday. But to think that he was who he was, and that he understood Owen—and that he was suggesting that she should talk to his mom!

He shrugged, looking a little embarrassed. "Are you back to thinking that I might be some creepy stalker, saying you should talk to my mom?"

She laughed. "Pretty much the opposite. I was thinking how amazing it is that any guy I just met would suggest that I talk to their mom."

He laughed with her. "I think we're getting off to anything but a conventional start here, aren't we?"

"Start? You see this as the beginning of something?"

He nodded. "I hope I don't freak you out—I hope you don't want to throw me out when I say this, but yes, I hope this is the beginning of something. You said you felt it, too, yesterday. There's something between us, something I'd like to explore—if you would?"

She nodded slowly. "It does sound crazy—but it feels right."
He smiled. "Then shall we see where it goes?"
She nodded again.

~ ~ ~

When they'd finished eating, Reid watched Tara clear the
dishes. She wouldn't let him do anything. Owen went back to
his room, and for the first time, Reid felt safe to ask about his
father.
"Is his dad still in the picture?"
Tara shook her head but didn't turn around, continuing to
load the dishwasher. "No. He wasn't able to deal with Owen.
He found it too difficult and so he walked."
Reid closed his eyes, wondering how any man could walk out
on their own child—and on their wife, leaving her to cope by
herself. When he opened them again, she'd turned around and
was looking at him. "I'm sorry." Was all he could think to say.
She smiled. "I'm not. It's better this way. Owen stressed him
out, which stressed me out. Me being stressed upset Owen and
so it was all just one big vicious circle. We were all unhappy
and exhausted. At least now it's just the two of us. Owen's
calmer, and I've found ways to make it work."
"You seem to make it work very well."
She smiled and waved her arm out, taking in the apartment.
"This is no palace, but we do okay. I wish we could go out
more—that's why I talked about Wyoming. Owen does well in
the countryside. I'd love to take him up there and live a quiet
little life."
Reid frowned, but didn't say anything.
She picked up on it. "You don't think that'd be good for
him?"

"It depends. I think it could be, but not if you just hid away with him."

"I know you're right, but it'll never happen anyway. It's just a nice idea. He loves dinosaurs and volcanoes. I like the idea of being up there near Yellowstone; I could show him the geysers and ..." she shrugged. "Like I said, it's just a dream."

"I wasn't criticizing. I think it's a good dream. I grew up just outside Yellowstone, in Montana though, not Wyoming."

"You did?"

He nodded. "It was good for me."

"What was it like?"

He smiled. "I had a great childhood. I had two big brothers to look out for me—and we didn't go to school, we were homeschooled."

She nodded. "That's my plan with Owen. I know the school system here. It wouldn't work for him, and the special needs system is just too overloaded. He's very bright. There's no way he could get the individual attention he needs."

Reid smiled. "You really should talk to my mom."

"I'd love to."

She seemed to have finished fussing with every little thing she could find in the kitchen. If he was right, she'd just been stalling because she didn't know what to do. He decided it was time to find out. He got to his feet and went to her, taking the dish towel from her hands and hanging it on the hook.

Her eyes widened as she looked up into his.

He put his hands on her shoulders and stepped closer. He didn't want to keep talking about her kid and his mom. He wanted to talk about just the two of them. He slid his fingers into her hair and tilted her head back. Her eyes fluttered closed as he lowered his head to hers. Her lips quivered as he brushed them with his. She stepped closer, and her arms came up around his neck, and he was lost. He slid his arm around her waist and held her to him. The feel of her warm, soft breasts against his chest spurred him on. He explored her mouth with his tongue, and she opened up to let him in. A kiss had never had this effect on him. His heart was pounding in his chest; his cock ached with a need he hadn't felt before. He pressed his hips against hers and let out a moan as she pressed back. His scalp and spine tingled as she sank her fingers into his hair and he wanted nothing more to sink himself inside her.

"Kisses."

They sprang away from each other at the sound of Owen's voice.

Tara looked terrified, which surprised Reid. He could understand that having the kid see them kiss might not be ideal, but it didn't justify the utter fear in her eyes.

"It's okay, Owen." She went to him and squatted down in front of him. "Reid was just—"

Owen smiled at her then looked up at Reid. "It's okay. It's nice. Reid's nice. Reid kisses Mommy. Reid loves Mommy."

Tara's cheeks flushed bright red. She shot Reid an apologetic look, but he smiled, wanting to let her know it was okay.

Owen kissed her cheek. "Owen loves Mommy." With that, he turned and went back to his room.

"I'm sorry." She looked embarrassed.

"Don't be. I'm just glad he didn't seem to mind."

"Didn't seem to mind?" She let out a short laugh. "I was afraid it was going to set him off. Remember how he was when your brother touched your shoulder this afternoon? That was nothing compared to how he gets when someone comes near me."

He hated the thought of anyone else going near her. "Does that happen much?"

She gave him a puzzled look. "No."

"I mean, do you date much?"

She shook her head.

He felt like an asshole. "I'm sorry. I'm getting carried away here. I want to be the only one you date."

She smiled. "You are."

He cocked his head to one side.

"This is the only date I've been on in three years."

"The only one?"

She nodded. "I know that sounds pathetic, but it's just how it is for me."

He shook his head. "Not anymore. We need to change that."

She laughed.

"I'm serious. This doesn't even count since we didn't go anywhere."

"It counts to me; it's been wonderful."

"It has?"

She nodded, and he stepped toward her again. Owen's interruption had served to confirm for him that he wanted to see her again—as much and as often as he could. And right now, what he wanted more than anything was to kiss her again—as much and as often as he could.

~ ~ ~

Tara closed her eyes and looped her arms up around his neck as he held her to him again. He felt so damned good. She felt so damned good when he kissed her. The feel of his hands on her back, the feel of his tongue inside her mouth. He made her feel like a woman—a woman who wanted a man to make love to her. He pressed his hips against hers, and she pressed back eagerly. His erection pressed into her belly. For the first time, she wished that Owen would stay with Nicole sometimes. She'd give anything to be able to take Reid into her bedroom, to get naked with him, to make love to him. She moaned into his mouth as one of his hands slid down to grasp her ass, pressing her against him so she could feel how much he wanted her, too.

When he finally lifted his head, her breath was slow and shallow. He smiled down at her, his green eyes still full of lust. "I want to get to know you better, Tara."

This time she was sure that he did mean in bed. "I do, too. But …"

He rubbed his thumb over her cheek. "It's okay. We can take our time."

She shook her head. "You're only here for a week."

"This time. I'll come back. Soon."

She nodded. She hoped he would, but she didn't dare to believe it was true.

"Come play."

They smiled at each other at the sound of Owen calling from his room.

"I'm coming," Tara called back.

"Reid!" Came his reply.

She looked at Reid, and he smiled. "Do you mind?"

"Mind? I think it's wonderful, just don't feel you have to. I need to spend time with him now, but if you don't want to …"

He reached out and touched her cheek again. "I do want to. I understand. You're a package deal."

She smiled and blinked rapidly, hoping to keep back the tears that were stinging.

"Did I say something wrong?"

She shook her head and sniffed. "No. You couldn't have said anything more right."

"Reid!"

He smiled, and she followed him to Owen's bedroom where he was sitting on the floor working on his dinosaur puzzle.

He'd completed it last night and then taken it apart again this morning. He must have done that puzzle hundreds of times, but he loved it. He held a piece up to Reid who sat down on the floor beside him.

Tara's heart filled up as she looked at them sitting there together. Reid took the piece, and Owen nodded at him. She tensed when Reid moved the piece to a place it obviously didn't fit. Owen started to get agitated. "No! No, no, no."

Reid smiled at him and moved the piece again.

"No!"

Tara wanted to step in and tell Reid to stop, but she got the feeling that he knew what he was doing.

"It's okay," said Reid. "It's okay to try other places."

Owen frowned at him. He looked like he was on the verge of a tantrum.

Reid moved the piece again and laughed. "Look, Owen, it doesn't go there, does it?" Owen looked at him, and he laughed again. "That's silly, isn't it? But it's okay."

Owen nodded uncertainly.

"Does it go here?"

"No." Owen sounded unsure of himself now.

Reid laughed again. "Of course not. That's silly, but it's okay!"

Owen nodded. "It's okay?" It was more of a question than a statement.

Reid nodded rapidly. "It's really, really okay." He slotted the piece into place. "That's where it goes."

Owen looked relieved. "That's where it goes."

Tara breathed a sigh of relief herself. When she and Owen did the puzzle together, she made sure she slotted each piece into its correct place immediately. He got so upset when things weren't as they should be.

Reid took the piece out again and put it in the wrong place. He laughed and nudged Owen. "It doesn't go there, does it?"

To her amazement, Owen smiled. It seemed he was getting the hang of the game Reid was playing. "No. It doesn't go there. Silly Reid."

Reid nodded. "Silly Reid. It doesn't go here either."

Owen watched him try to fit it in a couple other places.

"Do you want to try?"

Owen took the piece from him and studied the puzzle, then looked at Reid and smiled. "It doesn't go here." He pushed it into the wrong place and watched Reid's face.

Reid laughed hard. "You're so right. It doesn't go there! That's silly!"

Owen laughed uncertainly. "Silly." He looked up at her and smiled. "Reid's silly."

She nodded. "Reid is silly."

He looked up at her, and she smiled. He was silly enough to try to teach her son something that she'd never dared to try. She sat down with them and picked up a piece. "Do you think Mommy can be silly?"

Owen nodded happily.

She set the piece in the wrong place, and they all laughed.

"Silly, Mommy!" Owen picked up a piece and giggled as he put it in the wrong place. "Silly, Owen."

They spent the next half hour playing the new game of deliberately getting it wrong. They all laughed hard as they played. Reid would occasionally put a piece in its correct place and look at Owen when he did. "Oh, look, it goes there."

Owen nodded but carried on playing the silly game, which amazed Tara. Normally he couldn't stand it when things weren't right. Now he was more interested in having fun. She hadn't seen him laugh like this in as long as she could remember. Soon, his little eyes were starting to droop. It was past his bedtime, but she didn't want to spoil the fun—or end his new game on a sour note by making him stop and go to bed.

Reid let out a big yawn, making them both look at him in surprise. "I'm sleepy." He told Owen. "Are you?"

Owen nodded.

"Time for bed?"

Owen pushed another puzzle piece into the wrong place and giggled. "Silly!"

"Yes. Silly, but it'll still be silly tomorrow. I think it's time for bed now."

Owen nodded sadly. "Night night."

Reid shot a look at Tara, and she nodded.

"Why don't you let Mommy get you ready for bed, and I'll come and say goodnight when you're tucked in?"

He nodded again. "Night night."

Tara got him ready for bed as quickly as she could and tucked him in. "Did you have a good time tonight?" she asked.

"Yes. Reid's silly."

She dropped a kiss on his forehead. "He is. He's very nice."

"Very nice. Kisses. Reid loves Mommy."

Tara shook her head. That would be very nice, but it was hardly realistic. He was a wonderful guy, who was wonderful with her son—and who seemed rather attracted to her, but unlike Owen, she knew better than to think that a couple of kisses meant he loved her.

"Can Reid say night night?"

"I'll go and get him."

He was sitting on the sofa. For the first time, she realized how out of place he was here. Everything about him said he was wealthy; everything about her apartment said she wasn't. She pushed that thought aside as he turned and smiled at her. "Is he okay?"

"Yeah, he'd like you to say goodnight."

It was a weird feeling watching Reid sit on Owen's bed.

"Are you coming tomorrow?"

Reid looked at her. She didn't know what to say.

Owen looked at her, too.

"I'd like to," said Reid.

That was all she needed to know. "Yes, then. We'll see Reid tomorrow."

Owen smiled. "Night night, Reid."

"Night night, Owen."

Reid made to get up.

"Kisses?"

Tara blinked back tears as Owen reached up to Reid, and he planted a kiss on the little guy's forehead.

Owen placed his hands over Reid's ears and held them so he could look straight into his eyes. "You're silly," he said, then lay back down and turned on his side, pulling his sheet up over his shoulder.

They went back out into the living room, and Tara closed the bedroom door. "Thank you."

"It was my pleasure."

"You taught me as much as you taught him. I usually do everything I can to make sure I get the pieces in the right place as quickly as possible, so he doesn't get upset."

He smiled. "And that's what you'd think would be best. Except it just reinforces his need for everything to be in the right place. I wish the world worked that way, but since it doesn't, it's better to learn that it's okay when things don't go in the right place." He made a face. "For people like Owen—and me—it's never really okay, but if we can learn to accept it as silly and laugh when things aren't right, then life gets a lot easier for us."

She nodded. "I can see that now. I can't thank you enough. Even if you leave here tonight and we never see you again, you've given us both a huge gift that will help him so much."

He smiled and put his hands on her shoulders. "I do have to leave here tonight—even though I think you know I wish I could stay."

Her tummy flipped over when he said that. She wished he could stay, too. The warmth from his hands on her shoulders was washing through her and seemed to be settling between her legs. The heat that was building there had her aching for him to stay, but he was right, he couldn't.

"But I hate the thought of never seeing you again. Did you mean what you told Owen? Can I see you again tomorrow?"

"I'd love to."

"So would I. Shall I come here? What time?"

"Whenever you like." She didn't know if he meant for dinner—or what.

"He chuckled. How early is too early?"

She shrugged.

"How about I come at nine? We can go out somewhere?"

"That sounds perfect." She didn't have any plans. She'd be more than happy to spend the day with him—and she knew Owen would too.

"Okay then. I'm going to leave while I can make myself go." He rubbed his thumb over her cheek. "I want to kiss you, but I'll never go if I do."

She reached up and planted a peck on his lips. "That's all I dare to do."

"I'll see you in the morning."

She stood at the front door and watched him wait for the elevator.

"Goodnight, Tara," he said before he stepped inside it.

"Goodnight, Reid." She stood and watched the numbers above the elevator doors work their way down to the ground floor then went back in and locked her front door behind her. "Best night ever," she murmured to herself.

Chapter Eight

"Do you want to go out for lunch?" They'd spent the morning at Tara's apartment, playing with Owen and talking. It amazed Reid how easy she was to talk to. He'd learned a lot about her in the last few hours—she'd learned a lot about him, too. Normally, he was content to let other people talk. With Tara, it was different. She asked him what he thought, how he saw the world. He was happy to tell her. He was comfortable with her, and that was unusual for him—especially with a woman he found so attractive.

"I could make us a sandwich," she suggested.

"If you like—if that's easier?"

She shook her head. "We could go out, too. If I'm honest, I just don't know where to take you that would be up to your standards."

He cocked his head to one side.

"We've both been avoiding mentioning it, but we obviously live very different lives."

He knew what she meant. She meant financially. "Maybe so, but that doesn't mean we're different people. I'm happy to go wherever you'd usually go—wherever Owen feels comfortable."

She shrugged. "We don't often go anywhere. We'll risk the coffee shop sometimes, but that's about it."

"Let's go to the coffee shop then."

Owen clung to Reid's hand as they walked the few blocks. It made him happy. He and Owen had made an immediate connection in the same way he and Tara had. Reid knew it surprised her, but it didn't surprise him. He and Owen were much more similar than she realized.

He smiled when they turned the corner and he spotted the coffee shop. "That's Spider's place."

"You know it?"

He nodded. "I've only been here once, but I know Spider. He helps run the center. He and Grace have been friends for years."

She smiled. "I like that our worlds have at least some common ground."

"I think we have a lot more common ground than you realize, and we'll keep discovering more all the time."

She nodded, but she didn't look happy.

"Did I say something wrong?"

"No. You're probably right. I just don't see …" She shrugged. "It doesn't matter."

"It does. Something's bothering you, and I'd like to know what."

"I just … I like you. Owen likes you. This is great. But I have to be realistic. You're here for a week. You say you'll be coming back, but I have to think about Owen. The more time we spend with you, the more upset he's going to be when you leave."

"I know." He'd already given some thought to that. He knew that he shouldn't get involved with the little guy if he didn't plan to stay involved. The way he felt right now, he'd love to stay involved in their lives forever. But he knew that if he told her that it'd freak her out, and realistically, he'd need to spend more time with her before he knew for certain. He held the door open for her and Owen to enter the coffee shop ahead of him.

They took a seat in a quiet booth near the back. He was glad for Owen's sake that it wasn't too busy. "I'm not ignoring what you said. I understand, and I'm trying to find a solution. I want to see more of you both."

"Reid!"

They both looked up as Spider appeared at their table. "I thought that was you, but …" He smiled at Tara.

She smiled back. "But you weren't expecting to see him with Owen and me?"

Spider grinned. "Yeah. But this is awesome. How are you?" He looked at Owen. "How's it going, little buddy?"

Owen nodded solemnly. "You're not scary."

Reid laughed and gave Spider an inquiring look.

Spider laughed with him. "That's right. I'm not scary. I'm your friend."

"Owen thought Spider was very scary the first time we came in here," explained Tara. "But Spider sat with us for a while, and they became friends."

"That's right," said Spider. "We are friends, aren't we, Owen?"

Owen nodded happily.

"What can I get you guys?"

Once he'd taken their order, he smiled at them. "I'll get your drinks, and when it quiets down a bit, I'll come and catch up with you. You have to tell me how this happened."

True to his word, Spider came back to join them as they were finishing their sandwiches. "So, come on. Tell me how the two of you met?"

Tara looked at Reid, and he nodded. He was happy for her to explain it—partly because he was interested to hear her take on what had happened between them so far.

"We ran into each other when Reid was checking into his hotel, and I was there for a massage. Owen was upset, and Reid came to the rescue."

"Music," Owen told Spider.

Spider chuckled. "Music?"

"He gave Owen his iPod, and the music calmed him down."

Spider grinned at Reid. "Let me guess, that classical stuff you play all the time?"

Reid nodded. "It works for me. I figured it might work for Owen, too."

"And you were right." Tara smiled at him.

"And you've been seeing each other ever since? That's awesome."

Tara laughed. "It is awesome, but that was only yesterday."

"Oh!" Spider held up his hands. "Sorry, guys, so this is like a first date, and here I am putting you on the spot. Sorry. I'll leave you to it."

"It's okay," said Reid. "It's good to catch up with you."

"It's good to see you here again," said Spider. "Though I swear, I'm going to hold you to your word and come up to visit you one of these days. I've always wanted to see the San Juan Islands."

"I keep telling you. You're welcome any time. All you need to do is give yourself time off from this place and come."

"Thanks. I'm going to do it soon. I really am. I was watching videos of the whale watching tours again the other night. I want to do that so bad."

Reid laughed. "Then do it. Stop talking about it, and just do it."

"I will. How long are you here for?"

"Just the week."

"Okay. Well, if I don't see you before you leave, I'll call you. Thanks, Reid." He smiled at Tara and Owen. "It's good to see you. Come back and see me again soon, okay, little buddy?"

Owen nodded. "See you soon."

~ ~ ~

Tara enjoyed the feel of the sun on her back as they walked back to her apartment. The weather had cooled off over the last few weeks, and there was a hint of fall in the air.

She smiled as Reid took hold of her hand. She still had that surreal feeling, as if this was all just a dream and she'd wake up soon. "What do you want to do this afternoon?" he asked.

"Park."

She looked at Owen in surprise. "You want to go to the park?"

"With Reid."

Reid smiled at her. "Does that work?"

"It works for me, if it works for you."

"I'd love to." She was a little wary about it. She knew it'd be busy on a Saturday afternoon, but if Owen wanted to go, then she was hardly going to say no.

It was busy when they got there. Busy and loud. Kids were running around, laughing and playing. Families sat on blankets

or played ball games. Owen still clung to Reid's hand and
shrank behind him as a girl ran in front of them laughing.

"What do you want to do?" she asked Owen. She half
expected him to say he wanted to go home.

"Rocks."

She chuckled. Of course, he did. "Okay, then." She led the
way over to the edge of the playground to his favorite spot. He
loved to collect pebbles and pieces of quartz and then sit and
arrange them by size and color.

"Where are the rocks?" Reid asked him.

He led Reid to the edge of the path and started to pick up an
assortment of pebbles.

Tara watched as Reid joined in. She had to wonder what he
made of all this. He understood Owen so well, but she was
fairly sure that he wasn't used to hanging out with little kids.
Once they each had a handful of pebbles, Owen led Reid to
his usual spot and plonked himself down on the ground. Reid
sat beside him and watched as he began to sort them.

"Is this your favorite game here?" he asked.

Owen nodded and continued sorting.

Tara sat down beside them, then looked up at the sound of her
name being called.

"Hey, Tara!"

It was Deb. She was hurrying toward them with a big grin on
her face. This should prove interesting.

"Hi, Deb."

Deb gave her an exaggerated wink and shot a glance at Reid.
"Aren't you going to introduce me?"

"Sorry, yes. Deb, this is Reid. Reid, this is my friend and
neighbor, Deb."

Reid got to his feet and shook hands with her. "Nice to meet you."

"You, too. I saw you at the book drive yesterday. You're Reid Davenport, aren't you?"

He nodded.

"And I'll bet that was your limo outside the building last night, wasn't it?"

He nodded again.

Tara felt bad for him. She didn't know him well yet, but she imagined this was more than a little uncomfortable for him. To her relief, Deb didn't stick around.

"Well, I won't keep you. I just wanted to say hi." She grinned at Tara. "You call me when you get a minute. You know why."

"Will do." Of course, she knew why. Deb would want to know the whole story—and every detail.

"It was nice to meet you," said Reid. "I'll see you again."

Both Tara and Deb looked at him when he said that. He smiled at her. Apparently, he'd wanted to make a point, and he'd made it well.

"Don't like her," said Owen once Deb had gone.

"Owen!" Tara had to hide a smile. Deb had a good heart, but she wasn't really her kind of person, let alone Owen's.

Reid chuckled, and she just knew that he felt the same way as Owen.

"Go home now?"

"Okay, let's go." He wasn't upset. Apparently, he'd just wanted to share one of his favorite pastimes with Reid.

"Was that embarrassing for you?" Reid asked as they walked home.

"No. Not at all. I know she'll grill me when I see her again. But …" What the hell, she might as well say it. "It's hardly embarrassing for me to be seen with you. I know she's wondering how I managed it. I was thinking it was more embarrassing for you."

He chuckled. "I'm the one who wants to show off about being seen with you."

She looked up into his eyes.

He nodded. "It's true. You're right that Deb made me a little uncomfortable, but just because people mostly do. I'm happy for your friends to see us together. I'd like my friends to see us together, too."

"You would?"

"Yes. If you want to."

She nodded. She'd been trying not to think too far ahead. They barely knew each other yet, and she still wasn't convinced that they'd know each other at all after this week. She didn't want to set Owen up for disappointment, and she didn't want to set herself up either. "Maybe next time you're in town?"

He cocked his head to one side. "Not yet?"

"No."

"You think I'm not coming back?"

She nodded. "It's not that I don't believe you. It's just that ...""

She shrugged, hoping that he wouldn't be offended—or worse, tell her she was right.

"It's okay. I understand. You're right to be cautious—it's only logical. But for once in my life, I'm being the illogical one." He shook his head, looking slightly puzzled. "There's something much bigger than logic going on here."

Wow. She didn't know what to say to that. She didn't know what to make of what was going on between them. She liked the idea that it was something big and special—maybe something real and lasting, but that seemed too good to be true. She'd rather hold back and see what happened.

When they reached her building, Owen let go of Reid's hand and ran to the elevators. He pressed the button and watched the light above the doors as the elevator made its way down from the twelfth floor.

They rode up in silence. She was wondering if he'd leave now, or how long he planned to stay. She hoped he'd stick around while Owen took his nap. A shiver ran down her spine. She'd love to spend an hour alone with him. She kept remembering the way he'd kissed her last night. Her whole body tingled when she thought about it. It wasn't as though they could do anything—at least, nothing more than kissing again, but even that would be wonderful.

When she let them in, Owen went straight to the bathroom. She'd wondered whether he'd interrupt his routine because Reid was here, but apparently not. He came out ten minutes later in his pajamas. His hands and face were washed, and his hair combed. "Naptime," he announced.

"Sleep tight, little buddy," said Reid.

Owen smiled at him. "See you in one hour. No less." He repeated what Tara always told him when he went for his nap. He usually stayed down for an hour and a half these days, but he used to get up after ten minutes sometimes and then be cranky all evening. She'd taught him that this was his quiet time for at least an hour, and today she was grateful that it had become an integral part of his routine. It meant she was almost guaranteed a whole hour alone with Reid. She shivered again.

Once she'd settled Owen into bed, she came back out and closed his door behind her. When Reid smiled at her, it was different. The lust was back in his eyes. Apparently, he was thinking the same way she was.

She smiled back. "He wasn't joking when he said see you in an hour and no less."

"I believed him." He ran his gaze over her, and the heat started to build between her legs. "He's a great little guy. I'm enjoying spending time with him, but I'll be honest, I'm looking forward to having his mom to myself for an hour."

"What do you want to do?" She was turned on just by the way he was looking at her. If he said he wanted to take her to bed, she'd go willingly—despite her better judgment.

He smiled. "I can't tell you what I want to do—though I'm sure you could guess."

She nodded sadly. He was going to be the voice of reason for her, and she was grateful for it—though a little disappointed, too.

"It's too soon anyway." He sounded more like he was trying to convince himself.

"You're right, but I have to tell you. I wouldn't say no."

"That's good to know."

She laughed. "I'm sure it's obvious?"

"I was hoping I was reading you right."

"You were."

He patted the space on the sofa beside him. "Want to sit?"

She went and sat down, and he slung his arm around her shoulders.

"I don't know why you're wasting time with me. You could be with a child-free woman right now. I'm sure there are plenty of them who'd happily jump into bed with you this afternoon."

"I'm sure there are. But I'm not interested in a woman who'd do that. I'm not interested in a child-free woman. I'm interested in you." He brushed his thumb over her cheek and then tucked it under her chin, tilting her head back, so she was looking up into his eyes. "I wish I could jump into bed with you this afternoon."

She nodded. She couldn't look away from his deep green eyes that were searching hers.

"But I'm happy to wait for that."

She chuckled. "I can't say I'm happy."

"Maybe happy is pushing it. But I'd rather wait until the time is right. There's no rush. You said I'm wasting time with you. I don't see it that way. I feel like I'm investing time—in us."

Her breath came out in a big sigh as he tangled his fingers in her hair and drew her closer. She'd love for them to become an us. She'd love for this to be a beginning. She was starting to think it could be.

He brushed his lips over hers. They were warm and soft. It started out as just a sweet kiss, but she wanted so much more. She looped her arms up around his neck and drew him closer, wanting to feel his hard body pressed against hers.

The kiss intensified. He held her tighter as his lips crushed against hers and she sank her fingers into his hair. He moaned, just as he had last night when she did that. It turned her on so much. She lay back on the sofa, taking him with her so that he was awkwardly lying on top of her. He buried his face in her neck, nibbling and sucking. It was too much. She spread her legs, desperately wanting to feel him between them. She let out a needy little moan as the bulge in his pants pressed into the heat between her legs. He felt so good, but she wanted so much more. She rocked her hips wildly, realizing, but not caring that she was desperately dry humping him.

His hand had found its way under her top, and his fingers teased her nipple through her bra. She nipped his lower lip and wrapped her legs around his, needing to feel him against her.

"I want you, Reid," she breathed.

He lifted his head and looked down into her eyes. "I want you, Tara, but we can't."

She knew he was right, but she didn't want him to be. "We have an hour."

He closed his eyes in what looked like pain. "Don't tempt me. Please."

"He won't wake up. We can go in the bedroom and close the door." She slid her hand between them and stroked him through his jeans, knowing that would help her case.

"We can't," he said again.

She nodded sadly. "You're right. I'm sorry."

"God! Don't be sorry. You have no idea ..."

He got to his feet, and for a moment she wondered if he was disgusted with her for being so desperate. She should be disgusted with herself, but she was too turned on. It had been too long, and he was just so damned sexy. "Reid, I ..."

He shook his head. "I still don't think we should, but even just to make out, we should take it to your room and close the door."

She got to her feet, and he took her hand and led her to her room. Once they were inside, he closed the door behind them. "Do you lock it?"

"I probably should."

Once she'd locked it, she turned to see him sitting on the bed. He patted the space beside him with a smile, and she went to him.

Within a matter of seconds, he was on top of her again. She struggled with his zipper, just wanting to feel his hot hard cock pressing between her legs. Her skirt was up around her waist, so once she got him unfastened, there was only the thin layer of their underwear between them. She pushed his jeans down to his knees and spread her legs wider, needing to feel his hardness push into her soaking panties. He thrust his hips, and she moaned and began to move with him.

He rolled to the side, making her sigh with frustration. He was right, of course. Before she had a chance to speak, his lips came down on hers, and his hand stroked its way down over her belly. She clung to his shoulders and kissed him back as his fingers slid inside her panties. She tensed as he stroked her and circled her clit with his thumb. Then she bit down on his shoulder as he thrust two fingers inside her. His thumb worked its magic as he drove his fingers in and out. Her hips moved with him, bucking wildly, trying to draw him deeper. She didn't even last a minute. All her muscles tightened around him, and a white-hot ball of pleasure exploded, sending waves of pleasure crashing through her. His lips found hers, and he kissed her deeply as she came hard. There was something about that kiss—it was so intimate. He'd made her come, and now he was claiming her at her most vulnerable while her orgasm shook her.

When she was spent, she clung to him, still breathing hard.

"I could deny myself, but I couldn't deny you," he breathed.

She buried her face in his neck. "I'm sorry. I was all over you ... I couldn't. I shouldn't ..."

He titled her chin to make her look up at him. "Don't ever apologize for wanting me."

She smiled. "Okay then, I won't. But I owe you one."

He chuckled. "I'll hold you to that."

Chapter Nine

Reid made his way back to his room after breakfast on Sunday morning. He'd stayed at Tara's until late last night. It had taken every ounce of willpower he had to leave. They'd made out like horny teenagers again after Owen had gone to bed, and he'd been so tempted to make love to her. He blew out a sigh as he rode the elevator back up to his room. He was glad they'd waited, but he didn't know how much longer he'd be able to hold back. He stepped out of the elevator and walked down the corridor to his room. He always took a room as far away from the elevator as he could get. He disliked the noise it made—and the noise people made while they waited for it. An elderly couple emerged from their room and smiled politely as he passed. He smiled back. He wondered what their story was, why they were here. He imagined they'd been married fifty years or more. That made him smile. It made him wonder what that would be like. How would it be to share all those years of your life with someone? As he opened his door, he realized that he wasn't just wondering about someone; he was wondering about Tara. What would it be like to spend fifty years with her?

He shook his head. It was too early to even think about such a possibility. Yet here he was thinking about it. He didn't know her, but he felt as though he did. They'd only spent a couple of days hanging out together, but he knew who she was at her core. She was kind, she was practical, she was a devoted mother.

His phone rang, bringing him back to reality. He hoped it was her, but he doubted it. He'd said he'd call her at lunchtime— since he really needed to catch up with his brothers. They were, after all, supposed to be the reason he was here.

TJ's number flashed on the display and Reid smiled to himself as he answered. "Hello."

"Shit! If I wasn't worried enough about you before, now you're answering your phone like a mere mortal. What's she doing to you?"

Reid laughed. "I'm only playing with you. I couldn't resist. And I suppose I'm stalling too. I couldn't answer with the most appropriate information to your question because I don't know what the question might be."

"Either that, or you do know the question, and you don't want to answer."

Reid smiled but didn't say anything.

"The question is, what's going on with you and this Tara chick?"

"You already know. I went for dinner with her on Friday. I spent the day with them yesterday."

"And?"

"And what?"

"And what's happening?"

"I plan to see her again this afternoon."

"What about coming over here? I thought you came to visit with Dani and me?"

"I did, but …"

TJ chuckled. "Don't worry. Now I'm playing with you."

"You are?"

"Mostly. I was hoping we'd see you this afternoon. But I'm hardly going to stand in the way of your hot date. If you'd rather spend the afternoon in bed with her, then I'm not …"

"It's not like that." For some reason, Reid needed him to understand that this wasn't just about sleeping with some hot chick he'd met. "I haven't even …" Maybe that was too much information.

"Ah. Sorry. So. What's the score? What's going on with the two of you?"

"I like her. I like her a lot. I like her son, Owen, too. He's just like I was at his age."

"He is? Wow. So, this is serious?"

"It is. I don't know how serious it should be after just a few days, but … it feels very serious to me."

"Okay. In that case, I'll stop giving you a hard time. Do you want to bring her over here?"

Reid thought about that. "No. Maybe in a couple of weeks? It would be hard on Owen, and I don't want to put them under that kind of pressure. It'll be easier for everyone when we've been together a little longer."

"Okay. And you plan on being together a little longer? You're going to come back to see her?"

"I am. I plan on us being together a lot longer."

"Damn. I've never heard you talk like this before."

"Neither have I. It's interesting."

TJ chuckled. "Interesting? It's fascinating. Do you think she's your person?"

Reid stared out the window at the LA skyline for a few moments before he answered. "I do."

"Awesome. If you were anyone else, I'd tell you to be careful, to take it slow, but with you, I'm going to trust your judgment. You're smarter than anyone I've known. I'm sure you'll figure out what you're doing. But remember, I'm here if you want to talk about it. I know that's not your style, but ..."

Reid smiled. "Thanks, TJ. I might even take you up on that offer. It isn't my style, but then neither is falling in love."

"Shit! That's what you think you're doing? In a matter of what, three days?"

"I know. It sounds crazy. But if you describe most things I do, they sound that way. I'm not crazy; I just work differently."

"True, but ... I'm going to say it. Be careful. It's new territory for you. Love can knock you for a loop—and it can hurt like hell, too."

"I know. I intend to take it more slowly than I'd like."

"Good. So when will we see you?"

"Tomorrow? I'd like to come to the center. We need to talk about the bus, and I'd like to talk to Daquan again. I didn't get as much time as I planned on Friday."

"Okay, that sounds great. Do you want me to pick you up at the hotel?"

"Sure, what time?"

"Eight-thirty?"

"Okay, see you then."

Once he'd hung up, he went to the window and stared out at the city. Was Tara really his person? Something inside him—something that denied logic—insisted that she was. She and

Owen were meant to be in his life—he just knew it—and he was meant to be in theirs. But their life was here, and his was up on the island. Would she be open to moving there? Would it be fair to ask her? And was it premature to even consider it? He went through to the bathroom and washed his hands.

~ ~ ~

On Monday morning, Tara went through her usual routine with Owen. She got them both showered and fed, and then they spent some time reading his books. He'd picked up reading very quickly, and she was hoping homeschooling was going to work out for them. She was confident in her abilities as a teacher, but not so much in her ability to keep up with him.

He set the book down and smiled at her. "Mommy go to work now."

She nodded. One of her favorite clients had sent her his latest manuscript over the weekend. She was looking forward to getting started on editing it.

"When's Reid coming?"

She smiled. "I don't know yet. He's going to call later."

Owen frowned. "When's he coming?"

"I told you, Owen. I don't know." She'd been afraid of this. Owen was already getting used to seeing Reid every day. He wanted to know that he'd see him today—and at what time.

He started to rock back and forth. "Want Reid."

"And you'll see him soon."

"When?"

She blew out a sigh. "I don't know. And you need to be a good boy. Why don't you carry on reading while I get to work?"

He scowled at her for a long moment, and she was relieved when he nodded. "Okay."

She knew it was only a temporary reprieve. When she stopped for lunch, she knew he'd ask again. She hoped that Reid might call in the meantime and then she'd be able to answer Owen.

As she set herself up at her computer, she shook her head sadly, wondering if it was all worth it. She couldn't expect Reid to make arrangements in advance with her, just to keep Owen happy, but at the same time, she couldn't make Owen live in a state of uncertainty. It was the worst thing for him—and so it was the worst thing for her, too.

She opened up the book file and tried to focus on it. Usually, her work was her escape, but this morning she couldn't focus on it. She was too caught up in wondering whether she should tell Reid she couldn't see him anymore. It wasn't fair to any of them. But she wanted to keep seeing him. He'd told her he'd come back—not the coming weekend, but the one after. She was already looking forward to it, and he hadn't even left yet. Perhaps that was another reason she should just call it off. She shouldn't be wishing her life away, looking past her everyday life with Owen in her eagerness to get to a couple of days with Reid.

She stared at the screen, not seeing the words in front of her. If she told Reid she didn't think they should see each other again, Owen would be upset, but wouldn't it be better to upset him now than to let things go further—to let him get more attached and then have it end in heartbreak for him and for her? She shook her head. It was too soon to decide. Reid had said he saw this as a beginning, that he was investing time in them as an us. What might that look like, if they became an us, if this was something long-term—lifelong even? She smiled at the thought. She'd love for that to be the case, but it was crazy thinking. They'd only known each other for a few days.

She needed to get to work and stop wondering about it all. The only thing she could do was decide if she was prepared to take the risk. She was all in for herself. The possible reward of her and Reid ending up together far outweighed the risk of it not working out. But there was Owen to think about. The risk to him was much greater. She shrugged. She'd have to leave it to roll around in the back of her mind while she got on with her work. Her client had asked if she could do this one as quickly as possible, and she didn't want to let him down.

When she stopped for lunch, Owen was engrossed in his book. She set his sandwich down beside him, and he looked up with a smile and then continued reading. Usually, she made him come and sit at the table and eat lunch with her, but today it seemed worth letting him carry on. She still hadn't spoken to Reid, so she'd rather not have to answer Owen's questions about him.

She went back and sat down at the little dining table to eat her own sandwich. Her phone rang, and she grabbed it as fast as she could. She was hoping it was Reid, but whoever it was she didn't want it to ring long enough to disturb Owen.

It was Nicole.

"Hey, sis. How's it going? I'm not disturbing you, am I? Is this your lunch break?"

"It is." Tara smiled. She'd trained her sister well. "What's up?"

"I just wanted to check in with you—see what's happening with you and the sexy billionaire."

Tara laughed. "I don't think he's a billionaire."

"Maybe not, but he must be a multi-millionaire at least. And once you get that rich, what does it really matter? It's all just numbers once you've got more money than you need, right?"

"I guess."

"Well, do you think you're going to find out instead of just guess?"

"What do you mean?"

"I mean what's going on with the two of you? Is he going to sweep you off your feet and keep you in a style to which you could quite happily become accustomed?"

Tara laughed. "He's already swept me off my feet, Nic. He's wonderful."

"Has he literally swept you off your feet? Like, off your feet and into bed."

"No."

"Aww, I was hoping to get all the steamy details."

"Sorry to disappoint you, but there aren't any. We're taking it slowly."

"Slowly? I thought he was only in town for a few days? How long do you have left before he goes?"

"He's leaving Wednesday morning."

"Do you want me to take Owen so you can have some alone time?"

"No. Thanks. He and Owen get along really well. I told you that."

"I know, I was thinking more about you getting some time alone in the bedroom. No matter how well he gets along with Owen, you still need time for the two of you."

"I know, you're right, but …"

"I can send the girls to Steve's mom. Owen will do fine if it's just him and me."

"No. Thanks, Nic. I appreciate the offer. But it's okay."

"So, you're not going to sleep with him?"

"Probably not."

"Are you crazy? Oh … or are you just holding out so that he'll come back?"

"What do you mean?"

Nicole laughed. "I mean if you put out before he leaves, he might have got what he wants and not come back."

"No. It's not like that. He's not like that. It's just … well, if this is going to go anywhere, then there's no rush. And if it's not, then I'd rather not sleep with him and then say goodbye."

"You're so practical. If I were you, I'd be climbing all over him. I've been looking him up online—you landed yourself a hot one, sis."

Tara laughed. "He's gorgeous, isn't he? And I don't mind telling you that it's really hard not to climb all over him. We haven't done it, but we've come pretty close, fooling around."

"Now, we're getting to the truth."

"Yeah, I guess we are. If it weren't for Owen, we probably would have spent the whole weekend getting to know each other in bed."

"Damn, girl. And you're sure you don't want the chance to before he leaves?"

"I'm sure I do want the chance, but it's better to wait. See if he comes back."

"Well, you know best. But if you change your mind and you want me to watch Owen tonight or tomorrow night just call me, okay?"

"Thanks, sis. I will."

After she hung up, Tara thought about it. She couldn't send Owen over there tonight; he was looking forward to seeing Reid. But she could do it tomorrow. She could drop Owen over there and then have Reid spend the night with her before he left on Wednesday morning. It was tempting, but it was wrong. She knew she wouldn't feel right about it. And when she thought about what Nicole had said, maybe it was better to wait until Reid came back. She'd be so hurt if she slept with him and then didn't hear from him again.

Chapter Ten

"Thanks for everything you've done," said Grace.

Reid nodded. He hadn't done nearly as much as he'd planned to while he was here. His whole visit seemed to have been swallowed up by spending time with—or thinking about—Tara and Owen. "I'll be back the weekend after next. And don't forget, I'm happy to help with anything you need. Just let me know?"

"I will, thanks. And … you're coming back to see Tara?"

He nodded.

"Do you think this could be serious?"

He nodded again.

They both looked up as the door to Grace's office swung open, and Oscar came in. "Hey. I'm glad I didn't miss you. I got tied up at the club."

"I wouldn't leave without at least calling you."

Oscar grinned. "Not normally, you wouldn't, but this isn't a normal visit, is it?"

Reid shrugged.

"You know what I mean. You've been spending all your time with Tara and her kid. You didn't even call Mom on Sunday. You always call Mom on Sunday."

Reid sucked in a deep breath. That was right. He did always call home on Sunday. He often spoke to them during the week, too, but Sunday was the day he checked in with his parents no matter what. His mom worried if he didn't talk to her at least once a week.

Grace smiled at him. "You've had a lot going on."

"Yeah, but I should have called her. I need to call her." He looked at Oscar. "What did she say?"

"She asked what was going on with you. Of course, she thought I was being a bad influence, possibly holding you hostage so that you couldn't make it to a phone. I told her you met a woman and that you've been far too busy to even hang out with us."

Reid didn't know what to say.

Grace scowled at Oscar. "Don't you pick on him."

Oscar held both hands up. "I was only playing. You know that, right?"

Reid nodded. He did, but he still felt a little uncomfortable that he was apparently neglecting his family in order to spend time with Tara and Owen. "I'd better get going. I need to call Mom before I go over to Tara's."

"Are you going to stay the night there, before you leave tomorrow?"

Reid shook his head. He wanted to, but he had a feeling this evening might be difficult anyway. He had to tell Owen that he wouldn't see him for the next ten days, and he knew that wouldn't go down well with the little guy. He didn't want to risk making things worse if Owen somehow found him in bed with his mom. "No."

"Don't be so nosy." Grace was scowling at Oscar. "That's none of your business."

Oscar gave him a sheepish grin. "Sorry. I can't help it. I have high hopes for you."

Reid smiled. "No worries. So do I. I need to get going."

"Okay, say hi to Mom for me?"

Reid rolled his eyes. "I will."

When he got back to the hotel, he picked up his phone and then set it down again. He wanted to talk to his mom. He wanted to tell her about Tara and Owen. But at the same time, he was nervous. He'd never talked to her about a girl he was seeing before—he'd never seen the point. He didn't usually see a woman for long, and even when he did, the relationship usually had a predetermined start and end point—at least in his mind. He was good at assessing the qualities and flaws people had—and he knew himself very well, so he could tell how long he'd enjoy a woman's company before he needed to end it—or before he started to get on her nerves by being the way he was. It was difficult for most women to be with him. Like Dani had said, women wanted a man to understand their feelings. Not only that, they usually wanted him to anticipate and help them deal with their feelings, too. That was exhausting for him.

It was different with Tara. She wasn't looking to him to help her manage herself. She was too busy managing Owen. She'd carved out a niche for herself in life and was busy living it and making the best she could for herself and her son. She wasn't looking to him to make things better for her—emotionally or financially. But he knew he could make things better for her— for her and Owen, and he wanted to. He picked up his phone again.

His mom was the one who'd helped him find ways to live in the world. He wanted to do the same for Owen, and he knew he could use his mom's help. He had a feeling she'd be able to help Tara, too. He smiled as he dialed her number and waited. She'd be able to help her, and she'd probably fall in love with her.

"Reid! I was getting worried about you, darling."

"Sorry. I've been busy."

"So I heard."

He smiled. "Why don't you tell me what you've heard and then I only need to catch you up on what you don't already know."

She laughed. "Her name's Tara. She has a son named Owen— with whom you have a special bond. You've been spending every spare moment with her since you arrived in the city, and both your brothers are cautiously happy, while Grace and Dani are over the moon."

"That about sums it up."

"Are you staying there?"

"No. I'm going home in the morning."

"Oh."

He laughed. "You sound disappointed."

"I am. If the little boy is like you, then it's not going to be easy for him."

"I know. But I have to go home. I'm coming back next weekend."

She stayed quiet.

"What are you thinking? You might as well tell me."

"There's so much I want to say, but I shouldn't say a thing. I'm just getting carried away because of what your brothers have said."

"Tell me what you're thinking?"

"It doesn't matter what I'm thinking. I should let you go at your own pace and only offer my opinion when you ask for it."

He chuckled. "I am asking for it."

"My opinion doesn't really matter until I know how you feel about her. Where do you see this going?"

"I'd like to think …" He hesitated. Was he really about to tell his mom that he could see himself spending the rest of his life with a woman he'd known for less than a week? Yes. He was. "I'd like to think that she's my person."

His mom chuckled. "You'd like to think that she is, or you do think she is and you're afraid to admit it to me because you think it's too soon?"

"I do think she is."

"And for what it's worth, I don't think it's too soon. When you meet your person, you know. I knew Grace was it for Oscar the first time I met her and knew that Dani was right for TJ, too."

"So, how would you feel about meeting Tara?"

"You want me to?" She sounded surprised.

"I do. Obviously, it'd be reassuring to hear what you think, but even aside from that, I'd like you to meet her because I think you can help her."

"How?"

"Owen's just like I was when I was little. I can see him thinking all the same things I used to think, reacting in the same ways I did. Screaming the place down when things get out of sync for him. The other night he let me do his puzzle with him. As soon as I put a piece in the wrong place, he started to get upset, just like I used to. I played the same game you played with me. It was a struggle for him at first. It was weird; it was like looking back through time and seeing myself as a kid. But I remember the relief. I needed everything to go in its proper place, but you taught me that it was okay if it didn't." He laughed. "I still like things to be as they should be—"

His mom laughed. "Really? I hadn't noticed."

"Okay. I'm still pretty damned anal about things, but the way you taught me to play with that puzzle was the first big breakthrough I had. I'm hoping it can be the same for Owen, but there's so much more. I'd love for you to meet Tara and talk to her, help her. She's all on her own. She stays in almost all the time, works from home, never takes Owen anywhere he won't be comfortable and very seldom goes anywhere without him. I think both their lives could be better—whether I'm part of it or not—but she doesn't have anyone to turn to. You could help her. I know you could."

"You're such a good boy. You care about them very much, don't you?"

"I do. But I'd want them to be happy even if she wasn't my person."

"I know you would. I'd want to help her, too. But I think she is your person, isn't she?"

"Yes. She is."

~ ~ ~

"When's Reid coming?"

Tara gave Owen a stern look. He'd asked that question, and she'd told him the answer at least a dozen times in the last half hour.

"Seven o'clock?"

"Yes."

"Is that soon?"

"Yes, it's only fifteen minutes away now." She couldn't blame him. She was as impatient as he was for Reid to arrive. She wanted the minutes until seven o'clock to fly by, but then she wished that the minutes after seven could slow down somehow. They only had this evening left, and then he'd be gone for ten days. It was hard to believe that she'd grown so used to him coming around. This time last week she didn't even know he existed. Now he felt like an integral part of her life—hers and Owen's. She'd already explained to Owen that tonight would be the last time they'd see Reid until he came back to the city the following weekend. He hadn't been too happy about that, and she knew he'd be even less happy when tomorrow evening rolled around, and she had to explain it to him again. Maybe this was a bad idea.

She jumped at the sound of a knock on the door. He must be early. That made her smile. Until now, Reid had been spot on time—not a minute early and not a minute late. Maybe he was feeling the same way she was and wanted to make the most of all the time they had before he left. She opened the door with a smile. "Hey, you're early—" The words froze in her throat. It wasn't Reid; it was Mark. She knew her mouth was hanging open as she stood and stared at him. She couldn't help it. She hadn't seen Mark in over two years.

"Hey, babes. How've you been?"

Babes? He thought he could still call her by the pet name that he hadn't even used in the last year of their marriage? "What … what do you want?"

His smile faded. "I'm sorry. I should have called. I know this has to be a shock."

"Yeah. It's a shock, all right. We haven't heard a word from you in two years." She looked back over her shoulder. Owen had gone back into his room, and she hoped he'd stay there.

"I know. I was a complete asshole. I'm sorry. I couldn't cope. I couldn't deal with any of it. I … I'm sorry."

She shook her head. "There's no need to be sorry. It worked out for the best—for all of us. But you can't just show up like this. Owen …"

"How is he?"

"He's doing well."

"Can I see him?"

"Not now, no." She felt terrible saying that. She'd sworn to herself that she'd never stop Owen from having a relationship with his father. But she needed to prepare him for it. And now was not the best time. Reid would be arriving at any moment. Owen would be happy to see him. It'd be too much to have his dad here at the same time. They never even talked about his dad anymore. She sometimes tried, because she didn't want to be the one who kept a boy away from his father, but the boy had no interest.

Mark frowned. "Why?"

"Oh, come on! You can't still be so totally selfish that you don't understand? I'm shocked to see you, you've thrown me off. What do you think it'd do to him?"

Mark nodded reluctantly. "You're right. I'm sorry. But I want to see him."

"So, call me. Give me time to tell him and prepare him, get him used to the idea that he even has a father." She couldn't help getting that dig in.

Mark pursed his lips but didn't react. "Okay, but I want to see him, and I want to see you."

She shook her head. "I won't ever stop you from seeing him, and when you do, I'll be there. But you and me?" She shook her head again. "We're done."

"We don't have to be, babes. Don't you think it'd be better for Owen if he had both of us again? If we were a family again like we should be?"

Tara held his gaze for a long moment. There were so many things she wanted to say to that. But none of them mattered. They'd mattered three years ago, and he hadn't wanted to hear them then. Now, she no longer cared. "No. I don't. But like I said, I won't stop you from seeing Owen if you want to."

"I'll call you later."

"Call me tomorrow."

"Okay. What about this weekend, can I see you then?"

She looked back into the apartment, hoping Owen was still busy in his room. "We'll see. I need to go in. Goodbye, Mark." She closed the door in his face. She had to. She didn't want Owen coming out and seeing him there. She didn't think he'd even know who it was, but she didn't want to explain it to him. And she didn't want Reid to arrive in the middle of it. Owen would be thrilled to see him. Mark would be pissed to know she was dating, and no doubt even more pissed to see his son run to another man. She leaned back against the door and took a deep breath. Why did he have to show up now?

Owen came out of his room with a big smile on his face. "Reid!" His smile turned into a frown when he saw her standing there by herself. "Where's Reid?"

"He's not here yet."

"But ..." He must have heard her and Mark talking.

"That was someone else at the door. Reid will be here soon."

Owen scowled and went back into his room.

Tara held out her hands, they were shaking. How she wished that Mark hadn't shown up like that. She had no idea how she could integrate him into Owen's life. She couldn't imagine letting Owen go anywhere with him—and she didn't want to have to spend any time with the man. Especially now. She'd wanted to make the most of this evening—their last evening with Reid for a while. Now she knew she'd be distracted, worrying about Mark and what his intentions were. She whirled around at the sound of a knock on the door and peered through the peephole. It was Reid. She opened the door and forced a smile on her face.

He cocked his head to one side. "What's wrong?"

"Nothing. I … err … Oh, come on in."

He stepped inside and closed the door behind him before holding up a bunch of red roses. "I got these for you."

"Aww! Thank you so much!" She wouldn't have imagined him to be the flower-giving type, and that made the gesture even more special. "I should put them in water." She felt bad that she was using that as an excuse to take a few moments to gather her wits before she told him what was wrong.

Owen came out of his room and trotted toward Reid with a big smile on his face. "Reid's home."

Tara pulled a vase out from under the sink and tried not to let her mind go near Owen's words. Reid wasn't home. This wasn't his home. He was just here visiting—before he left town. She knew that. She might wish like Owen did that his home was here with them, but it wasn't. It was a thousand miles away.

She put the flowers in water and then turned back around. Reid had taken a seat on the sofa, and Owen was sitting beside him. They both looked so earnest. Reid was leaning forward, his elbows on his knees and his hands grasped together. Owen was mirroring him, with his little feet sticking out in front of him. They were adorable together. She wished that Reid was Owen's father. But he wasn't. And Mark was.

"Want to tell me what's wrong?" he asked.

She shook her head. She could hardly tell him while Owen was sitting there. "Later. I was thinking we could go for a last walk to the park." She hadn't been thinking that at all, but at least if they went out she'd be able to tell Reid about Mark without Owen hearing. She didn't think she could stand sitting here and not being able to say anything.

Reid looked puzzled but nodded. "Okay. Do you want to go to the park?"

Owen shook his head.

Tara's heart sank. She didn't want to get into an argument about it. To her relief, Reid stepped in.

"Please? I want to see the stones again."

Owen's brow furrowed while he looked Reid in the eye and thought about it. "Okay," he said eventually.

Chapter Eleven

Owen clung to Reid's hand as they walked to the park. He'd already grown to love the way he did that. If he was honest, he'd grown to love everything about the little guy. Perhaps it was because he could see so much of himself in him. He understood him and wanted to help him, to make life easier for him.

He shot a glance at Tara. He needed to know what was wrong with her. She obviously had something on her mind. She smiled at him, but it wasn't her usual easy, relaxed smile. She was agitated. Upset about something. That bothered him. He didn't have her down as the type to get upset easily.

When they reached the playground, Owen led him toward the pebbled area, and they each collected a handful. He wanted to leave him to play by himself, but he wasn't sure how that would go down. He got to his feet with a smile. "I'm going to make sure Mommy's okay." To his relief, Owen was so engrossed in sorting his pebbles that he nodded and didn't even look up.

"I'm guessing you didn't want to tell me what's wrong in front of Owen."

"Yeah. I'm sorry. I didn't want to upset him." She looked upset herself.

He sat down on the bench beside her and leaned his weight against her, hoping that it felt reassuring. His heart started to race when a thought occurred to him. Maybe she'd decided that she didn't want to see him anymore. He tried to concentrate on returning his heart rate to normal. He wanted to tell himself that it was an illogical conclusion to jump to, but it wasn't. He could see that she might think it would be better for Owen if he weren't in their lives anymore. He knew that when he left, it would be difficult for Owen—and therefore for her, too. "What is it?" He tried to keep his voice even.

She didn't look at him but watched Owen play instead.

The suspense was killing him. He had to ask. "Have you decided that we're over?"

She swung her head to look at him. "God, no! No. Not at all."

He smiled as a wave of relief surged through him. "Sorry. You had me worried there."

"I'm sorry. It didn't occur to me that you'd think that."

He shrugged, feeling foolish. "I couldn't help it. You've been so distracted since I arrived. You wouldn't tell me what's wrong. I thought maybe you were building up to a goodbye." He curled his arm around her shoulders and hugged her into his side.

"No. I don't want to say goodbye to you."

He dropped a kiss on her lips. "I hope you never do."

She shook her head. "You might change your mind about that when I tell you what's bothering me."

He frowned. "What is it?"

"Just before you arrived, Owen's father showed up."

Reid cocked his head to one side. He didn't know how to process that. "I thought you didn't see him anymore."

"We don't. We haven't seen him; I haven't spoken to him for two years. We've been divorced for three. The first year he made some efforts to keep in touch with Owen. Not much, but he'd come over on Saturday mornings sometimes ..." She shrugged. "It was too much effort for him, and it slowly petered out. He hasn't even called in over two years."

Reid shook his head. He didn't know what to say to that. "And what does he want now?"

She closed her eyes and drew in a deep breath before slowly blowing it out again. "He said he wants to see Owen, and that he wants us to be a family again."

Reid had gotten used to feeling his emotions physically when he was around her, but up to this point, those feelings had all been good. Right now, he felt as though he'd been punched in the stomach. "I see."

She looked into his eyes. "No, you don't see. That's not what I want. We were a family at one time, and it just doesn't work. He can't handle Owen, and I can't handle him. I lost all respect for him the way he walked out. I know it's tough, it's tough for me, too. But ..." She shook her head. "You don't just walk out on your own son because it's hard to handle."

Reid nodded. He couldn't agree more, but he didn't feel like it was his place to say so. A man who could walk out on his wife and child, especially under those circumstances, didn't rate as much of a man as far as he was concerned.

"I'm not in any turmoil over him for my own sake. I'm upset because of Owen. Mark doesn't know how to handle him, so if he wants to see him, I'll have to be there. Owen doesn't know him anymore. He was too small to really even remember him. I don't want to go through it, to put him through getting to know the man, having to deal with him. I'll be honest with you, I doubt Owen will even like him—and that's going to be tough for everyone to deal with."

"It is." Reid knew it was going to be tough for him to deal with. Since he'd met Owen he'd seen him as a little kindred spirit, a child he could help and mentor. He had been seeing himself filling the father role in Owen's life—and he'd liked that. He didn't see himself being the interloper with another man's son. But the other man wasn't good for Owen … "So, what are you going to do?"

She shrugged. "I told him to call me. I need time to figure it out." She looked into his eyes. "What I wish I could do is tell him to go screw himself. He chose to walk away from us, and he can stay gone. Owen doesn't need him; I sure as hell don't need him. But … I can't bring myself to do it. He's Owen's father. I would never want to be that mother who keeps her child away from his father."

Reid nodded. He knew she wouldn't do that. Even though it would probably be better if she did. Doing the right thing wasn't always the right thing. He could hardly tell her that though. He was biased anyway. He didn't want the guy near her or near Owen.

She was watching Owen again. "He has the worst timing, too. Why did he have to show up now?"

"What's worse about now?"

She gave him a small smile. "I'm already bracing myself to cope with Owen when you leave. It's going to be hard for him."

"I'm sorry."

"It's not your fault."

He felt like it was.

"It's just going to be two big upheavals for him at the same time. You're going to leave, and Mark's going to come into his life. And knowing Mark, he won't stick around for long anyway. He'll want to see Owen a few times, and then when he gets the message that I'm not interested in taking him back, he'll move on again."

"You really think so?"

She nodded. "I might be wrong. He might genuinely be interested in building a relationship with his son, but even if he is, I doubt it'll last. It'll be too hard for him, and he'll give up."

"Can I do anything to make it easier?" If she wanted him to, he'd stay. He almost suggested it, but he didn't want to come off as the territorial male, sticking around because there was another man in the picture. If he stayed, it would be for Owen's sake, to provide some stability. At least that was what he wanted to believe.

"No, thanks. I can't ask you to do anything, other than please just bear with me? I have a feeling this is going to be a tough run."

"Anything you need, anything I can do for you and Owen, I want to be there."

~ ~ ~

Tara wished he could be there—literally, physically stay here with them. It'd help Owen, it'd help her, not to mention the fact that she'd love for him to stay. But she couldn't ask that of him. It was too soon. If they'd been dating for a few months, she might have asked him. It'd be the best solution.

She had a feeling that Mark would back right off if he knew there was no chance of getting back together with her.

She smiled. "How do you do with listening to ranting females?"

He raised an eyebrow.

"I have a feeling I'm going to get angry about this. I'm going to need to let off some steam. So, if you don't mind me calling you and just venting?" She worried as soon as she'd said it. She didn't want to come across as a needy or bitchy type. She wasn't one. She'd been trying to let him know that she wanted to be open with him, that she'd tell him all about what was going on. But judging by the look on his face, he wasn't too impressed with the idea.

"I don't mind." His face belied his words.

She chuckled. "That's okay. You look horrified. I can vent to my sister. It's just that I know I'll hear all about what an asshole he is from her—that and how stupid I was to ever have married him."

He hugged her closer to his side and dropped a kiss on her lips. "You misunderstood. It's not that I don't want to be there for you, to listen. It's more that I want to be here for you."

She gave him a sad smile. "But you can't be."

She couldn't figure out the look on his face. He looked like he was going to say something, but instead he just nodded.

"Reid!"

They both looked at Owen who was walking back to them holding both his hands out. When he reached them, he rested his little hands on Reid's knees, palms up, each containing a piece of quartz.

"One for me, one for you."

Tara's eyes stung with tears. How she wished that this could be straightforward. Why couldn't it be Reid saying he wanted them to be a family? That wasn't fair. Maybe he would want that, someday, down the line. But right now, that didn't help. She knew she had a rough few weeks ahead—and Owen did, too.

When they got back to the apartment, things felt different between them. It made her sad. Reid was distant somehow, and she didn't like it. He was still the same with Owen, but while the two of them sat on the sofa looking through Owen's book, she kept catching him glancing at her while she made dinner. He'd offered to bring something for them to eat, but she'd wanted to cook for him.

When Owen went to the bathroom, she went and sat down beside him. "What is it?"

He shrugged. "I'm sorry. I guess I keep thinking about what might happen with you and Mark."

"There's nothing to worry about. I have no interest whatsoever in getting back together with him. I've told you. I'm glad he left."

"I know, but he's Owen's father."

She shook her head adamantly. "Only biologically. You've been more of a father to him in the short time you've known him than Mark ever was. Listen, I know it's too soon to say this; I don't want to put you under any pressure, but I hope that someday you might want to be his dad."

He rubbed his thumb across her cheek. "It's not too soon. It doesn't feel like pressure. It feels like reassurance. I already do."

She stared at him. He meant it. She could tell by the look in his eyes. She leaned forward and kissed him. It was only a brief kiss; she didn't want Owen to come back out and catch them, but that kiss felt like it sealed things between them.

When she leaned back, he smiled. "You call me whenever you want and let off as much steam as you want."

She laughed. "I don't want to put you off by making you think that I'm an overemotional female."

"I already know you're not. I just want to be here for you."

She held his gaze for a long moment. There seemed to be so much meaning to his words. She got back up when Owen came out. She felt better. She still wasn't looking forward to dealing with Mark or Owen once Reid left, but at least now she was looking forward to being able to talk to him and to tell him all about it.

After they'd eaten, they all went and played the getting it wrong game with Owen's puzzle. It still unsettled him a little a first, and a couple of times she caught him slotting a piece into its proper place when he thought they weren't looking. Reid spotted it too and smiled at her. It was a moment that she knew would stick with her. Up to this point she hadn't been able to share little moments like that with someone who understood her son. She smiled back, wanting to take his face between her hands and kiss him senseless.

When Owen was ready for bed, they both sat with him for a few minutes. Tara's eyes filled up as she watched him reach up and take hold of Reid's ears, so he could look him in the eyes in the way that had already become so familiar to her. "Night night, Reid. See you tomorrow."

Reid glanced at her. She'd hoped this wouldn't happen. It'd be easier for her to deal with it tomorrow—once Reid had gone. She couldn't let it go though. She knew that if she let him go to sleep believing he'd see Reid tomorrow, it would be even more difficult when he couldn't.

"Reid has to go home tomorrow," she reminded him.

Owen scowled at her. "Reid is home."

Her heart hammered in her chest. She wished that was true just as much as he did.

"I have to go back to my other house," said Reid. "I'll be back though."

"When?" Owen was scowling at him.

"Ten days." He looked deep into Owen's eyes. "Can you count to ten?"

"Pft." Tara wanted to laugh at the contempt in the little sound he uttered. "One, two, three, four, five, six, seven, eight, nine, ten."

Reid chuckled. "Well, it won't be quite that fast, but let's make a chart with ten days on it, and you can cross them off."

Owen wriggled out of bed and Tara didn't have the heart to stop him. He came back with a piece of paper and a crayon and Reid wrote out all the days from tomorrow, Wednesday, until next Friday when he'd return. Then he numbered them from ten to one. "Maybe you and Mommy can mark them off each day when you go to bed? Each day will tell you how many more there are until I come back."

Owen nodded sadly. "Ten days?"

"Ten days."

Owen blew out a big sigh. "Okay. Kisses?"

Reid planted a kiss on his forehead and then Owen turned and landed one on his cheek. "Kisses. Reid loves Owen. Owen loves Reid."

Tara covered her mouth with her hand and tried desperately to blink away the tears. She felt like her heart must overflow seeing the two of them like that.

Owen reached out to her, and she couldn't help it. She hugged him tight until he wriggled free. She kissed his cheek, and he smiled. "Owen loves Mommy."

"And Mommy loves Owen."

"Night night," he called when they reached the door.

"Goodnight, Owen. Love you."

Tara bit her lip, struggling to believe that she'd somehow gotten so lucky to find a man like Reid.

~ ~ ~

When she'd closed the door behind them, Reid hugged her to him. "I should go."

She looked up into his eyes. "You don't want to stay?"

"That's the trouble. I do. You know I do. But after saying goodbye to him like that, it'd be even worse if he wakes up and finds me still here. If I stay for even a few minutes, I'll be here for the night."

She looped her arms up around his neck, and he let out a sigh as she pressed the length of her warm, soft body against him.

It felt like an invitation. He'd love to take her up on it. But it wasn't right. He knew he had to go. The next ten days would be telling. If her ex hadn't showed up, he might have decided not to go home tomorrow. But he had to give the guy a fair go. Although Tara denied it, Reid believed there was a chance—however slim, that she and Mark could get back together. He hated the idea, but he had to let it play out. If Owen could be with his biological father, then he shouldn't get in the way of that just for his own selfish reasons.

He lowered his head and brushed his lips over hers. She kissed him back with a passion that almost made him forget reason and logic. Almost. He was breathing hard by the time he lifted his head. He stepped away from her reluctantly. "I'll see you next Friday."

She nodded sadly. "Will you call me when you get home? Let me know you made it?"

He smiled. She sounded like his mom—and that reminded him. "I will. And I'll call you every night—if you want."

"I want."

"I forgot to tell you that I spoke to my mom. Would you like to talk to her? Can I give her your number?"

She nodded. "If she doesn't mind? Maybe it's not a good idea?"

He brushed his thumb over her cheek. "She thought it was a wonderful idea."

"Okay."

He made his way to the door and then stopped to kiss her again. He tried to let her know without words how much he was going to miss her—and how much he hoped she'd still want to see him when he came back.

"I'm going to miss you," she said.

"I'm going to miss you, too."

She blew out a sigh. "If this is it, if you decide not to come back, I just want you to know that it's been wonderful."

He tightened his arms around her. "The only reason I wouldn't come back is if you tell me not to."

She reached up and planted a kiss on his lips. "I'll see you next Friday then."

Chapter Twelve

"Are you sure you don't want me to stay?"

"No. I'd love you to stay, Nic, but it'd just make things worse. You and Mark always antagonized each other."

"Yeah. And I'd be happy to antagonize his ass right back to where he came from."

Tara had to laugh. "I know, and I wish I could let you. But he's Owen's dad."

"So? You wouldn't give him this much leeway if he was just a sperm donor, and he's no better than one."

"I know. You're right. I'm not going to argue with you, but it's not about him. It's about doing what's right. I don't believe you should ever keep a child from knowing his father."

"Hmph! Would you say that if he was a murderer?"

"He's not a murderer, though."

"Yeah, but my point is where do you draw the line between doing what's considered right and doing what's best for your kid?"

Tara shook her head. "It's best for a child to know his father. I believe that."

"Well, I believe you're giving too much importance to the fact that Mark was your sperm donor. If Owen wasn't his biological son, you wouldn't even consider it. If he was someone you met and started dating you wouldn't even let him meet Owen."

Tara rolled her eyes.

"Exactly! You wouldn't even date him because now you're old enough and wise enough to see what an asshole he is. At least your taste's improved. Reid's a real catch. I wish you'd tell Mark to go screw himself and just focus on you and Reid."

"I wish I could too, but …"

"Argh!" Nicole was so frustrated she was turning red. "I want to give you a shake and make you see it. But I know I can't. So, I'm going to leave, but you call me as soon as he's gone, okay?"

"Okay." She gave her sister a hug. "I have to do this."

"No, you don't. I wish I could get that through to you. You don't have to do this at all. It's going to upset Owen. That's the only thing I see coming out of it."

Tara knew she was right. She wasn't looking forward to Mark coming over. But she couldn't make herself tell him no. She truly believed that a child and his father had the right to know each other. She closed the door after Nicole and went back inside.

Owen was sitting on the sofa. He had Reid's iPod gripped tightly in his little hand, but he wasn't listening to the music. The earbuds sat on his lap.

"You don't want Bach?"

He scowled at her. "I want Reid." He'd said that every five minutes since he woke up on Wednesday morning.

She felt the same way. "I know. We'll talk to him on the phone later."

"I want Reid." He started to sway back and forth, which was never a good sign. She was hoping he'd at least be calm when Mark arrived.

"I know, Owen. I do, too. But it's only a week till we'll see him now, and we can talk to him tonight. After your dad's been to visit."

He scowled again. "Don'ton't like him."

She sighed. He'd been saying that ever since she'd told him that Mark was going to come and see him. Usually, he followed it with I want Reid. "You don't know that, sweetie. You need to get to know him. He's your father."

His little face was set and stubborn as he shook his head. "I don't like him." He put the earbuds in and stared determinedly in front of him.

Tara got to her feet. Conversation over, she muttered to herself. She felt the same way Owen did; she couldn't blame him. She wished that Reid was here and that Mark had stayed gone from their lives. Unfortunately for her, she was a grown-up, and she couldn't just dig her heels in and choose to listen to music instead. She had to deal with it.

She didn't hurry when she heard the knock on the door. She walked toward it with a sense of dread. This wasn't going to go well. She knew it.

Mark smiled when she opened the door. "Hey. Thanks for this. I know it's a shock to you, me coming back. But you won't regret giving me another chance."

"All I'm giving you is the chance to get to know your son."

He held up a bunch of flowers. "I know I'm going to have to work for it." He smiled. "I got something for Owen, too." He opened the plastic bag he was carrying and showed her a big yellow fire engine. It was one of those that had a siren and flashing lights—and was everything that would set Owen off the wrong way.

"I don't think that's a good idea. It'll be too much noise and—"

Mark pursed his lips. "You'll just have to deal with it." He walked past her into the living room. "Hey, Owen. Remember me?" He took the fire engine out of the bag and held it up to show him. "Want to play?"

Owen looked up at him, and the furrows deepened on his brow. "No."

"Come on. It'll be fun." Mark pressed a button, and just as Tara had feared, a siren started wailing.

Owen looked at Mark as if he were a three-headed monster. He looked at the fire engine and back at Mark before he scrambled off the sofa and ran screaming to his bedroom.

"Shut that thing off," Tara snapped as she followed Owen and closed the bedroom door behind them. He was curled up on his bed, rocking back and forth, staring, unseeing out the window. "It's okay, sweetie. He'll make the noise stop."

Owen didn't reply. She didn't expect him to. He was gone, hiding in his own world, somewhere deep inside himself. She sat on the bed beside him and hugged him. She couldn't help it. He usually pulled away from physical affection, but sometimes she just needed to hold her little boy and try to reassure him. He leaned his cheek against her side for a moment and then sat up. It was enough. She'd reached him. She tried to blink away the tears. Maybe Nicole was right? If this was what having Mark around was going to do to Owen, how could it be right? She blew out a sigh.

"I want Reid."

She swallowed—hard—and nodded. "So do I, sweetie. Do you want to come and see your dad? He's turned the siren off now."

"No. Don't like him."

"Okay." There was no point in trying to make him. She knew that. "I'll go and tell him."

Owen nodded. He was still clutching the iPod.

"Do you want to sit here and listen to the music?"

He nodded again and pressed play.

Tara drew a deep breath before she opened the door and went back into the living room.

Mark looked ashamed of himself. "I'm sorry. I didn't think."

"Obviously."

"Tell him I'm sorry. Is he coming back out?"

"No. He needs to calm down. He needs some quiet time."

Mark waggled his eyebrows at her. "Great. So, we get some quiet time, too?"

"No. We get some time to talk."

"Okay. What do you want to talk about?" He sat down on the sofa and patted the space beside him.

The gesture made her think of Reid. She loved it when he did that. With Mark it just made her go and take a seat at the dining table.

"We need to talk about what you're playing at. About why you've shown up again now."

He gave her a sheepish grin. "I know I'm fucking it up, but I meant what I said, babes. I want us to give it another shot. I've been doing a lot of thinking lately. I was an asshole to you and Owen, and I want to make it up to you." He looked around her apartment. "You deserve better than this. And I can give it to you. The two of you should move in with me. You shouldn't have to struggle."

She let out a short laugh. "I wouldn't struggle so much if you made any sort of contribution."

He hung his head. "I know, and I'm sorry. Like I said, I want to make it up to you."

"Then start paying child support. But don't think that we're going to get back together. We're not. If you want a relationship with Owen, we can try to make that happen. But honestly, I'm not sure that it's a good idea. You don't know the first thing about him—or you don't care. You should've known that a toy like that would set him off."

He shrugged. "I thought he'd be better now he's a bit older."

She laughed again. "Is that why you're back? You thought maybe he'd grow out of it and things would be easier now? Because believe me, they're not."

He shrugged again. "Yeah. I suppose I thought he would have grown out of it a bit. At least now you can talk to him, tell him off when he acts up like that. He needs to learn."

Tara closed her eyes. "This isn't a good idea, Mark. I think you should go."

"Don't do that, Tara. I'm just being honest. I can learn. I'm his dad. I'll get the hang of it."

She nodded sadly. She wasn't sure he would, but those three little words—I'm his dad—triggered something inside her. She knew what it was. She and Nicole had grown up not knowing their dad. Their mom had refused to talk about him, right up until the day she died.

"I think you should go. We'll try this again. Maybe you can come one night next week after work."

"But I'm off all weekend. I thought the three of us could hang out."

"No. He's tired, and he's upset. We got off to a bad start. How about Wednesday?"

He pursed his lips. He was going to argue. She knew it. "Look. I mean it. I'm not interested in us getting back together. I'm not going to change my mind about that. So, maybe it's best if you take a few days and think about whether you really want to be part of Owen's life. Because if we do this, that's all it's going to be. I don't want to put Owen—or us—through all the upheaval if that's not what you want."

He smiled and came toward her. "But babes—"

"Don't call me that!"

"Let me guess? There's someone else, isn't there? I'm not stupid. I know you didn't buy those yourself." He pointed accusingly at Reid's roses standing in the vase in pride of place on the dining table.

She shrugged. "That's none of your business. It's not about whether I'm seeing someone. It's about the way you walked out on us and the way I had to build a life for Owen and me. I don't want you back."

He made his way to the door and stopped when he got there. "I'll call you about Wednesday. You can't keep Owen away from me." He slammed the door on the way out.

Tara blew out a big sigh and Owen came out of his room with big frightened eyes. "It's okay. He's gone."

Owen nodded and went and sat on the sofa. "Don't like him."

~ ~ ~

Reid sat at his desk and stared out at the ocean. It calmed him. Something about the incessant motion helped his mind to be still. He knew that Mark was going to see Tara and Owen tonight, and it had him unsettled. She'd reassured him that she wasn't interested in the guy—and he believed her. That wasn't his biggest concern. He was worried about Owen. He was doing okay. They'd talked on the phone every night, and Owen had told him each time how many days were left until he returned. It was difficult, though. In the few days he'd been with them, Owen had been happy with the new routine. When he'd left, he'd disturbed that routine, and now Mark was another upheaval. It wasn't good all coming together like this.

He tried to focus on the ocean—on the movement—but his mind didn't want to be still. He wanted to pack a bag and go back to LA, even though that would make matters worse at this point. He'd told Owen ten days, and if he showed up again before that, Owen would be pleased to see him, but still thrown off by the unpredictability that was being introduced into his life. Reid remembered all too well how hard it had been when he was a kid. He'd needed everything to be predictable. Changes in his routine were unbearable. He'd come a long way since then. He found ways to cope—and ways to make sure that he could keep core parts of his life running to a predictable, comfortable schedule.

He picked up his phone. He wanted to talk to his mom. She was the one who'd figured out how to make his life bearable. And he was hoping that she might have spoken to Tara—or that she would soon.

"Hello, poppet," she answered.

It made him smile that she still called him that, though he knew his brothers struggled with it more than he did. "Hi, Mom. How are you both?"

"We're doing well. We just made the trek to Montana. We're going to be here for the next few months."

"You're there early this year."

"Yes. I was missing the mountains. And your dad has such a great staff at the clinic now that it was easier to persuade him to come away."

Reid laughed. "He'll still go back a couple of days a week."

"He will; he's going on Tuesday. And while he does, I'm going to LA for a little shopping."

"You mean you're going to check how Oscar and TJ are doing?"

"Well, I might have dinner with them. And I was thinking I might call Tara and see if she'd like to have lunch with me. What do you think?"

"She might. Don't ask her to go to any of your usual places though. She won't feel comfortable to bring Owen, so she'll say no."

His mom laughed. "Remember who you're talking to? I was thinking I'd suggest Spider's coffee house. He said the three of you have been there."

"You talked to Spider?"

"Yes. He's a very sweet young man. I do like him. He's been a good friend to Grace."

"He has. But how …? Never mind." Reid wasn't sure he wanted to know. His mom befriended all kinds of people. He should hardly be surprised that she was buddies with Spider. "That's probably a good idea, and if she says no, just suggest you can go and see her?"

"She wouldn't think I'm being too pushy?"

"She might, but I doubt it. She knows that you understand how hard it can be to go anywhere."

"I do. I'm looking forward to meeting her. Do you think you might bring her up here?"

"I'd like to. I know she'd love for Owen to see the park."

"I'm sure it'd do them both good, and maybe, once she gets to know me—and of course, once Owen does—she might let me watch him so the two of you can go out for dinner."

Reid smiled. "Thanks, Mom."

"You're most welcome, dear. You know I'd love it if you came to live here."

"Live there?!"

"Yes. If she really is your person, and I believe she is, then the two of you are no doubt going to move in together. I know you wouldn't be able to live in LA, and I doubt it's the best place for Owen to be. It'd do him good to be here, just like it did you."

Reid nodded. He didn't know what to say. He'd been thinking about Tara in terms of forever, but he hadn't dared assess the possibilities of what forever might look like.

His mom laughed. "Your dad would tell me I'm getting carried away, but time isn't much of a factor. When you know, you know, and you might as well get on with living your happily ever after."

"I'd love to see his face if he heard you say that."

She laughed again. "And I'd love you to see his face if you asked him about our whirlwind romance."

Reid cocked his head to one side. It surprised him to realize that he didn't know how his parents had met or what their relationship had been like—or how long it had lasted—before they got married. "I might oblige you there and ask him next time I see him."

"Ooh, I hope you do. That'll be fun. Anyway. I should go. I'll give Tara a call now, and I'll let you know what we arrange."

"Thanks, Mom"

Reid straightened the collar of his polo shirt as he hung up. He should perhaps have told her that now was a bad time. Perhaps. But he didn't dislike the thought of Tara taking her call while Mark was there.

Chapter Thirteen

Tara was nervous as she pushed open the door to the coffee shop. It was kind of Reid's mom to offer to meet with her. It would be good to talk to someone who knew what it was like to raise a child who was different. But still. It was weird because the child she'd raised was Reid. Tara had no doubt that she'd be curious about her. She hoped she'd be as nice as she sounded on the phone. She took a deep breath as she looked around—she was about to find out. Owen clung to her hand and looked around, too. He seemed less nervous than she was. He liked the idea of meeting Reid's mom. It seemed he liked the idea of anything to do with Reid.

A woman in her fifties got to her feet and waved. "Tara?"

Tara smiled and made her way over to her table. "Hi. Yes, I'm Tara, and this is Owen."

"It's lovely to meet you both. I'm Jean." She wrapped Tara in a hug that made her want to hug back and stay there a while.

Jean let go and bent down to Owen's eye-level. "Hello, Owen."

"Hello." To Tara's relief, he smiled.

Jean slid into the booth. "Where would you like to sit, Owen?"

He slid onto the bench next to her. Tara sat down opposite them. She was a little surprised—but pleasantly so—that Owen had chosen to sit next to Jean.

Spider came out and smiled around at them. "What can I get you?"

Once they'd ordered, Jean smiled at Owen, and he smiled back. "Are you Reid's mommy?"

"Yes, I am."

"Reid loves Owen."

Tara was just glad that he hadn't said Reid loved Mommy.

Jean smiled. "I know he does. He told me."

Tara didn't know what to say. She didn't know what Reid had told his mom about the two of them, but by the looks of it, he'd told her quite a bit.

Jean smiled at her. "I'm not a nosy old bat, I promise."

Tara laughed. It was such an unexpected thing for her to say. "I didn't think you were."

"Good. It can't be easy for you meeting your boyfriend's mom when he's not even here."

Tara shrugged. She hadn't been thinking of this as meeting her boyfriend's mom so much as meeting someone who'd raised a child like Owen. "I'm glad you wanted to."

"I did—and not to interrogate you about you and Reid. He told me that he thought I might be able to help."

"That's what he told me, too. Though I don't even know what to ask. Owen and I live a quiet little life. We have it figured out."

Jean nodded. "Figured out in that you don't go anywhere unfamiliar or do anything that he isn't used to?"

"Yeah."

Jean sighed. "That's how my husband wanted to do things with Reid, too. On the surface, it makes sense. You keep a small controlled environment, and you can manage how it affects him." She smiled at Owen who was watching her. "It works for the short term, but it only creates problems in the long term. You can't shield him all his life. And believe me, I know you want to."

Tara nodded.

"With Reid, we homeschooled him and his brothers, but then we had them join in with extra-curricular activities. It worked well."

"I can see that it would up there in Montana, but I'm not so sure about doing that here. I plan to homeschool him, but I don't know about taking him to after-school clubs."

"Yes. It would be different here. Have you considered moving away from the city?"

"I'd love to, but it hasn't been an option."

Jean smiled kindly. "You never know, that might change."

Tara smiled. Was Jean imagining her moving away to be with Reid? She couldn't say she hadn't thought about it—as a distant possibility.

"Take for example, where we are in Montana—where Reid grew up. It's a very different life. The schools are smaller. The whole community knows each other." Jean smiled. "I think that—or somewhere like it—would be good for Owen, and for you."

"I imagine it would."

Spider returned with their drinks and sandwiches and set them down. "How are we, ladies?"

"Great, thanks," said Tara.

Owen smiled at him. He was in good spirits today. "I'm not a lady."

Spider laughed. "I know. You're my little buddy, right?"

Owen nodded. "And you're not scary."

Jean laughed at that. "I thought Spider might be scary when I first met him." She spoke to Owen but winked at Spider.

Owen nodded at her. "He's big and painted."

Tara laughed. He was talking about the tattoos that covered Spider's arms.

"He is. But he's very nice and very kind, too."

Owen nodded again. "Like Reid. Nice and kind."

Tara's heart melted. Reid was nice and kind. He was also strong and sexy and … she stopped herself. She shouldn't be thinking about him like that in front of his mom.

Spider grinned at them. "When's he coming back?"

Owen scowled. "Friday, three more days. Dad's coming back tomorrow. One more day. Don't like him."

Tara's heart started to race. She'd told Owen that Mark was coming to see him again on Wednesday and had used the same countdown tactic, hoping that, although that was something he wasn't looking forward to, at least having the timeline set out for him would make it easier. Spider was giving her a questioning look, but Jean was smiling.

"Reid told me you saw your daddy."

Owen didn't look happy at all. "Don't want to see him. Want to see Reid."

Tara nodded at Jean, wishing she could explain. "Owen hasn't seen his dad for a long time and now …"

Jean reached across and patted her hand. "I know. Reid told me all about it."

Tara was relieved. She didn't want Jean to think that she was seeing Mark while Reid was gone.

Spider frowned at her. "I thought he was out of the picture."

"So did I, but he showed up again, and he wants to see Owen."

"Owen doesn't want to see him," said Owen.

Sometimes she wondered if he followed the conversation around him. In this case, he was following it closely and making his opinion known.

"Do you want to come and choose a cookie for after your sandwich?" asked Spider.

Owen nodded eagerly and looked at Tara.

"Okay." She knew Spider was trying to give her a few minutes alone with Jean. Though what she was going to say to her, she didn't know.

Jean smiled as she watched Spider take Owen behind the counter and lift him up to look in the display case. "It must be hard," she said. "It's easy for me to spout advice, but I had Johnny to help me. You've done it all on your own."

"I have, and I wish it could stay that way." Tara regretted the words as soon as they came out. "I mean. I wish Mark had stayed gone. I don't mean Reid. I wish …" She shut her mouth before she said too much.

Jean smiled. "It's okay. I understand. I wish, too. That you and Reid …" She shrugged. "Since you're not saying it, I won't either. But I can hope. What are you going to do about Mark?"

Tara shrugged. "Honestly, I'm just hoping that he'll change his mind again. He came back saying he wanted another shot with me. But I made it clear. Even if I hadn't met Reid, there's no way I'd ever get back together with Mark. But I can't keep Owen away from him … can I?" She almost wished that Jean would say yes, she could, and that, in fact, she should. That would make things so much easier.

Jean sighed. "You're too big of a person to keep him away from his father. But you don't think his father's good for him, do you?"

"He isn't. He doesn't understand Owen, and he doesn't want to. He thinks he just needs a firmer hand—that he can be taught to behave."

Jean let out a short laugh. "He is behaving—in the only way he knows how." She smiled. "If you were to move away, do you think Mark would make the effort to come and see you?"

Tara met her gaze and shook her head. "I doubt it very much."

"Sometimes, with people like that, you need to put the onus on them. They want what they want—until they have to get off their ass to get it, then they don't want it anymore. If you were happy here, then I wouldn't suggest leaving to get away from him, but since you can see yourself being happier elsewhere, then it might just be time to go."

Tara nodded. Was Jean really suggesting that she and Owen should leave the city to be with Reid and that that would solve her problem with Mark? It certainly sounded that way—and she loved the idea. But there was the small matter of what Reid might think about it.

~ ~ ~

On Tuesday evening, Reid paced the living room. Tara had gone for lunch with his mom this afternoon, and he was waiting to hear from her about how it had gone. He wanted to call Tara and ask her, but they spoke later in the evening—just before Owen's bedtime.

He could call his mom, but that seemed irrational. She'd said she would call, and she would when the time was good for her. She could be doing any number of things, enjoying her time in the city. What bothered him the most was that this was so unlike him. He didn't get impatient; he didn't pace the floor waiting for news. He knew that everything happened in its own time and was content to wait. Usually.

He went to the bathroom and washed his hands, looking himself in the eye in the mirror as he did. He wanted to ask himself what was going on, but he knew the answer. He had to smile. It was Tara. She had him completely turned around. And for the first time in his life, getting the right answers was more important than getting an answer at the right time. He'd heard people talk about love—and thought it was a strange concept. He'd been able to rationalize it that people could somehow, instinctively recognize a compatible mate. He knew that both of his brothers were in love. Now that he'd witnessed it, he was less sure there was any rational explanation. At least not one that could be explained within the scope of current research on—what? Would the explanation be neurological, psychological, or physical? All of the above. He chuckled. What he did know was that both Oscar and TJ were in love. And if he wanted to draw comparisons or conclusions, he would go so far as to say that he, too, was in love.

He dried his hands on the soft towel and nodded. Tara was like a soft towel. She felt good against his skin. And the way she felt calmed him and soothed him. But more than the sense of physical touch, she made him feel. Emotions. He couldn't explain it, but he knew that he wanted more of it. Being around her made him happy.

She was strong. He admired that about her. She was positive, too. In his experience, too many people preferred to focus on the negative in their lives—and it had the effect of perpetuating the negative. He couldn't stand to be around people like that. They drained his energy, and he had no capacity for empathy with them. He was sure that many women in Tara's situation would focus on all the negatives— and feel justified in doing so. She'd been dealt a rough hand. She simply made the most of her situation. Dealing with Owen wasn't easy, but she did the best she could. Being alone had to be hard for her. She had no support—not financially, not emotionally.

But his feelings for her went way beyond respect and admiration. He smiled, perhaps that was where the physical element came in. He'd felt a strong physical attraction to her from the first moment he'd laid eyes on her. A shiver ran down his spine as he remembered the physical intimacy they'd shared. It hadn't been enough, not nearly enough. But it had been more pleasurable to him than any of his other physical encounters. He'd believed sex was about two people assisting each other in their quest for pleasure. And, damn, had he been wrong about that! He'd slept with his fair share of women, but he'd never experienced anything like he had with Tara. With other women, he'd experienced orgasms and had enjoyed himself—obviously. But with Tara, he hadn't even entered her, hadn't even gotten there himself, yet it had been more intensely pleasurable than anything he'd known before.

He blew out a sigh. There was no way he'd be able to hold back when he saw her again. He'd planned to arrive back in the city on Friday lunchtime but had decided he'd go to the center before he went to see her. He knew if he was there in the afternoon that they'd make the most of Owen's naptime. He didn't want their first time to be a quickie with them both keeping an ear out for Owen the whole time. He wanted to get there in the evening. Play with Owen and wait until he was asleep before he took Tara into her bedroom. He closed his eyes and drew in a deep breath. His cock was aching at the thought of finally being naked with her. He wanted to touch and taste every inch of her. He could hear the little moans she'd made when he'd spread her open and thrust his fingers into her. He cupped his aching balls as he imagined spreading her legs and finally thrusting his hard cock deep inside her wetness.

He jumped guiltily at the sound of his phone ringing and hurried out to answer it. He knew it'd be his mom. He chuckled at the thought that, love wasn't the only unexplainable human instinct. He had to believe that mothers also possessed inexplicable instincts—instincts that made them check on their sons whenever they were alone with an erection! He knew a survey of teenaged boys the world over would confirm his suspicions.

"Hi, Mom."

"Hey, poppet. I'm not disturbing you, am I?"

He tried not to laugh. "Nothing that can't wait. How did it go today?"

"It was lovely. Owen's a little sweetheart, isn't he?"

"He is."

"And Tara ..."

He waited. He could tell by her tone that she liked her, but he wanted to hear all the angles she'd come up with. She saw the world so differently than he did; he knew she'd see something he hadn't.

"I adore her, Reid. I think she's it for you."

He smiled. "I do, too."

"You're not holding back, or wanting to take it slowly and make gradual methodical progress?"

He laughed. "No. I'm not. I'm as surprised as you are, but I want to be with her. I acknowledge that there will be a learning curve. I'm sure we'll both discover things about each other that aren't ideal, but the big picture is, I think I'm in love with her."

"You think you are?"

"Give me a break, Mom. Acknowledging that love exists and that I can feel it is a big enough leap. I assess and evaluate everything with my mind, so, yes, I think I'm in love with her. To me, saying that is the same as someone else declaring that they have fallen in love. The difference is just semantics."

His mom laughed. "Very true, and I believe Tara will understand that. Her experience with Owen has taught her that just because we express ourselves differently, it doesn't mean we're not feeling the same thing in our own way."

"That's true. She has been more understanding and accepting of me and my ways than any other woman has been. But don't worry. I have enough experience with women to know how to express it in a way that will feel good to her."

"I know. I was only teasing you. And I have to say, I hope your experiences with women—as you so daintily put it—are behind you now. Oscar was bad enough. I never expected you to be quite the Casanova you were."

He laughed. "Casanova? That's pushing it, Mom. I've had a few girlfriends. That's all."

"Hmm. And you've had a lot more short-lived and very physical friendships. I know. Anyway, that's not a conversation we need to be having."

Reid silently nodded his agreement.

"My point was that I hope you and Tara are going to get together for the long-term. She's wonderful. She's strong and smart and soft all at the same time. She has a big heart and a lot of grit. I'd be proud to have her as a daughter-in-law."

Reid cocked his head to one side. "A daughter-in-law?"

"Yes. Don't go coy on me. I know you too well, poppet. You can't have decided that you're in love with her without having considered all the implications. You love her, you marry her, you make a little brother and sister for Owen, and you all live happily ever after."

He laughed. "So you've mapped out the rest of my life?"

"Haven't you?"

"I haven't given it a timeline yet."

"I'm only teasing. You should take it as slowly as you like—or go as fast as you want. There are no rules."

"I know. I'd love to go fast. But for Owen's sake, I think we should take it slowly."

"I was going to say that for Owen's sake, you should speed it up."

"Why?"

"He doesn't think much of his father, does he? And he's not very happy that he's going to visit them again tomorrow."

"I know. I'm not thrilled about it either. But he's Owen's dad. I can't stand in the way of that."

"Then maybe you should consider what I suggested to Tara."

"Which is …?"

"I'm not an interfering old bat, you do know that, don't you?"

He laughed. "If you are, you're a very well-intentioned one."

She laughed with him. "That's not nice. In fact, I might not even tell you now."

"You know I'm only teasing. What did you suggest? I'd love to hear it because Mark is the one cloud I see on our horizon."

"Me too, that's why I suggested that Tara might want to move her horizon ... to somewhere like Montana."

Reid cocked his head to one side. "To get away from Mark?"

"For many reasons. I think it would do Owen and her good to get away from the city. I think life in the valley would be good for both of them. She's too good a person to stop Mark from seeing Owen if he's just around the corner. But I get the impression that Mark isn't that good of a person that he'd make the effort to see his son if it involves doing more than dropping in on a whim when it suits him."

Reid smiled. "I think you're right about that."

"People split up and move away all the time. It happens. It wouldn't be anything out of the ordinary. I feel bad saying it, but I think he's a manipulator, and with people like that you have to be smart. If he really is interested in Owen, then Tara can agree to make as much of an effort as he does. But I think we'll find that he won't go to any trouble at all."

"You're sneaky, Mom."

"No. I just want to see her happy, and by the sounds of it, I think Mark could make her and Owen very unhappy. Sometimes you just need to remove yourself from people like that, so they can't make you miserable."

"What did she say?"

"She didn't say much, but I think she liked the idea."

Reid liked it, too. "I'll ask her about it when I call her tonight."

"You do that. I need to go, but I'll call you when I get back to Montana. Maybe we'll see you up there soon."

He smiled. "Maybe you will."

Chapter Fourteen

"Hey, Reid." Terry wheeled into TJ's makeshift office in the storeroom at the center. "What are you doing here? I thought you were coming to see that sweet girl of yours."

"He is." TJ smirked. "I think he's just come to check in with us, so he doesn't feel bad about ignoring us for the rest of the weekend."

"Not true. I won't feel bad about it." Reid made a face at his brother. "If it weren't for Tara, I wouldn't be back in the city at all. And besides, I'm not just here for the weekend. I'm going to stay a while."

"How long?" asked Terry.

Reid shrugged.

TJ eyed him suspiciously. "Don't expect me to believe that you're going to play it by ear. That you don't have a plan. I know you."

Reid chuckled. "Obviously, I have a plan, but I'm not in charge of the timeline. There are other factors that will dictate how long."

Terry grinned at him. "Are those factors named Tara and Owen?"

Reid nodded. "Yes, they are."

"But I don't see you staying here," said TJ. "It doesn't suit you. You need to get out of the city after a couple of days."

"I do, but I don't plan to spend the whole time in the city. I'd like to take them up to Montana."

TJ grinned. "Are you going to catch up with Shane? Show him that his lessons have served you well and that you've landed yourself a good one?"

"I will try to catch up with him, but mostly it's about seeing how Owen and Tara might like it there."

"You have a house there, same as him and Oscar, right?" asked Terry.

"I do. I haven't spent any time there for years, but ..."

TJ gave him a puzzled look. "I thought you'd be more interested in taking her up to see San Juan island—and the house you live in, rather than the one you don't."

Reid shrugged. "It wouldn't work for them there, but I think Paradise Valley might. Owen could have the same kind of childhood we did."

Terry grinned at him. "So, you're planning a future with 'em, are you?"

"I hope so."

Reid smiled as Oscar tiptoed in and surprised TJ when he put a hand on his shoulder.

"For fuck's sake!" TJ spun around, but Oscar just laughed. He'd been sneaking up on TJ like that ever since Reid could remember—and it pissed TJ off that despite all his military training, Oscar could still surprise him.

"What's going on, guys?" Oscar asked.

"Reid's just honoring us with his presence before he goes off with Tara," said TJ.

"Goes off with ...?" Oscar raised an eyebrow at Reid.

"He's taking her to Montana," said Terry with a grin.

"Wow! That's awesome. Do you want to use the plane? Grace and I are staying home this weekend. Woody can take you if you want. He just called; he's got nothing going on. I'll bet he'd take you tonight if you want to go."

Reid cocked his head to one side. He hadn't been planning on going to Montana this weekend. He'd just arrived. He planned to stick around for a while and then when they had a good routine going, he thought he'd take them up there. But ... why not? It made sense. Why get settled into a routine and then disturb it to take a trip? Why not take the trip first? That way both he and Tara would have a better idea if Montana was going to be a possibility for them. "Thanks. Do you mind if I let you know tonight? I need to talk to Tara first. We wouldn't leave until tomorrow."

"Sure, whenever."

"Thanks."

Reid smiled to himself. He hoped Tara would like the idea—and that Owen would be okay with it. But he couldn't think about going anywhere tonight. It'd be too much—for all of them. And besides, he already had a plan for this evening, and it involved Owen being tucked safely in his own bed—while he got Tara into hers.

"Are you sticking around here for a while?" asked Oscar. "I thought you'd be going straight to her place."

"I will get going soon. I just wanted to check in with you guys first."

"Well, I'm here to try and drag Grace away from her desk. So, I'll see you soon, I hope, and call me if you want the plane? In fact, let me know either way?"

"Okay. I'll call you later."

TJ looked at him once Oscar had gone. "Why do I get the impression that you're just biding your time until you can go to her place?"

Reid didn't want to tell him the truth. He straightened his collar and shrugged. "Maybe because I feel like a spare part here? There's nothing I can usefully do, and I'm not good at just standing around chit-chatting."

Terry chuckled. "You've done your bit, shown us your face. Go see your girl."

Reid smiled. He could always rely on Terry to be supportive. "Thanks. I think I will. How's your girl?"

Terry gave him a mysterious grin, and TJ laughed.

"I'll tell you about it when I see you again." Terry made a face at TJ.

"And if he does, be warned that Oscar and I will hold you down till you spill what you know, just like when we were kids. Whatever's going on between Terry and Barbara, he's playing it close to his chest." TJ turned a hard stare on Terry. "And we all want to know."

Reid laughed. "Don't worry, Terry, you can tell me, and I won't tell a soul."

TJ nodded. "It's true. He could survive all kinds of torture and never tell a word. We used to hold him down, tickle him, all kinds of things."

Terry laughed. "In that case, I'll look forward to catching up with you."

Reid looked around when he got out of the cab outside Tara's building. It wasn't a terrible part of town, but he'd be happy when he could move her and Owen away from here. He wondered what she'd think of his house in Montana. He wondered how he'd feel about living there. He nodded to himself. He liked the idea.

"Reid?"

He stopped and looked back over his shoulder, surprised that someone was calling him. He didn't see anyone he recognized until she called again. It was Tara's neighbor, Deb. He straightened his collar and plastered a smile onto his face. Hopefully, he'd be able to keep this brief—very brief. "Deb, isn't it?" He smiled politely.

She grinned as she caught up to him. "It is. I'm surprised you remembered. I'm Tara's neighbor."

He nodded and waited to see what she had to say.

"Are you here to see her?"

He nodded again. He would have thought that much was obvious.

"How are you two doing?"

He cocked his head to one side. He wasn't used to being asked about his personal relationships by strangers. To be fair, she wasn't a complete stranger. She was Tara's friend. They might be close, though he doubted it. "Great, thanks." He started walking again, hoping that might be the end of the interaction, but she fell in step beside him as they made their way into the building.

"I'm glad. She's a good person. She deserves to meet someone like you." She pursed her lips. She wanted to say something else. He could tell.

He waited, and after a few moments, she nodded, as if she'd made her decision. "I probably shouldn't say this …"

Reid shook his head. Why did people do that?

"You know Mark's been around again?"

Now she had his full attention. "I do."

She smiled. "I know. I wasn't trying to tell tales on her anything. She told me that you knew."

Reid smiled back; he was warming to her a little.

"It's just … He's bad news, that one."

"In what way?"

She shook her head. "He's been running with a bad crowd. Dealing. I don't know if he's using, but I'd put money on it.

I'm worried about Tara and little Owen. I don't think they should be around that."

Reid nodded his agreement. "Thanks for telling me. Have you told Tara?"

She blew out a sigh and shook her head. "I wanted to make sure it wasn't just rumors, first." She gave him a sheepish grin. "Honestly, I've been snooping on him. The guy's bad news. After he and Tara broke up, he lived with a girl I know for a while, and he was a bastard to her kids. I don't trust him as far as I could throw him. When I saw him back in the building the other night, I asked Tara what was going on." She chuckled. "I have to tell you, I was pissed at her—I've already dreamed up a fairy tale ending for her with you."

Reid smiled. This woman wasn't his kind of person, but she had a kind heart, and she cared about Tara, and that was good enough for him. "To tell you the truth, I have, too."

Deb's hand flew up to cover her mouth, and her eyes grew wide. "You have? Oh, my God! That's awesome! Oh, you just made me so happy. She deserves someone like you. She really does."

Before Reid knew what was happening, she'd wrapped him in a bear hug and squeezed him tightly. She looked embarrassed but thrilled as she stepped back. "Sorry, I couldn't resist. I'm just so happy." Her smile faded. "But that's all the more reason you need to run Mark off. I'm telling you, he's bad news."

"But he's Owen's father."

Deb's brows knit together. "I told you, don't listen to Tara on that one. It means nothing. He's not fit to be around kids. He's worse than she thinks he is. You need to get her and Owen away from him. Nothing good's ever going to come of having him in their lives."

Reid straightened his collar and nodded. "Thanks for telling me. Obviously, I'd like them to have nothing to do with him, but I didn't feel I should have a say."

"Well, you can forget any noble ideas you might have had about doing the right thing. The right thing is making sure he doesn't go near them. Just run him off."

"Thanks."

They'd reached the elevators, and Deb pushed the button. She smiled at him as they waited. "I imagine you'd want to take her away from all of this anyway."

He nodded.

"Then do it. Give her and Owen the life they deserve, and never look back."

They got in the elevator, and Reid wondered what he could say to let her know how glad he was that he'd run into her and that she'd told him.

When they stopped at the eleventh floor, she smiled. "This is me."

He held the door open with his foot after she stepped out. "Thanks, Deb. I can't thank you enough."

She smiled. "You can. You can send me a wedding invite." She started to walk away, then turned back and laughed, just as the doors were closing. "Or you could introduce me to one of your friends?"

He laughed with her as the doors closed. He would if he could think of someone. Maybe when he and Tara got married, someone he knew would be taken in by her. She might be a little rough around the edges, but right now she was one of his favorite people in the whole world.

A few moments later, he stepped out on the twelfth floor and hurried to Tara's door. He couldn't wait to see her and Owen and to get started on their future. A future he was more relaxed about now that he felt justified that he could put their main obstacle behind them.

~ ~ ~

Tara hurried to the door when she heard the knock. Owen came scurrying after her. Reid was finally back. She opened the door and caught her breath at the sight of him. He was gorgeous. His green eyes seemed alive and happy as he smiled back at her.

"Reid's home."

They both looked down at Owen, and he beamed back up at them. This might be the happiest she'd ever seen him.

Reid reached down, and she wasn't even surprised that Owen held his arms out and let Reid scoop him up. He curled his other arm around her waist and dropped a kiss on her lips. It was only a chaste peck, but it sent shockwaves running through her. She'd been looking forward to him coming back so much it hurt—or at least it ached, in all the good places.

"Kisses," said Owen and he planted one of Reid's cheek.

"I missed you guys."

"We missed you, too,"

Owen nodded. "Stay home now?"

Reid nodded, and the way he smiled made Tara wonder what he was thinking. He held her gaze. "I think it's time we figure out what we're going to do about home."

She raised an eyebrow at him, but he just smiled back. He was letting her know there was something on his mind. But he knew it'd be better to wait to discuss it until Owen wasn't listening in.

They went through to the living room, and Owen wriggled to get down. He ran into his bedroom, and Reid closed his arms around Tara's waist. She melted against him and pecked his lips, wishing it was bedtime already—Owen's and theirs.

Shivers chased each other down her spine as he tangled his fingers in her hair. "Do you want to go to Montana?" he murmured.

Her heart started to pound in her chest. Ever since her lunch with Jean, she'd kept daydreaming about the life they could have if the three of them moved to Montana. She'd been hoping it might be a possibility, but she certainly hadn't expected it this soon. He couldn't mean it? Not yet? She looked into his eyes.

"I saw Oscar while I was at the center, and he offered us the plane for the weekend. I said I wanted to take you up there so you can see how you like it ..." His smile faded as he watched her face. "We don't have to if you don't like the idea."

"I love the idea!" How could she tell him that she looked disappointed that he wasn't asking her to move there?

"But ...?"

She smiled. "I'm just surprised. That's all. When would we go? How do you think Owen will cope with it?" She realized as she asked that it felt natural to ask his opinion about Owen. That surprised her, and it didn't at the same time. She was so used to having to face everything alone, to not listening to other people's opinions about her son. But it was different with Reid; he was different. He understood Owen, and he understood her.

"It'll be as difficult as any new experience. But it's something I'd like us to do at some point. Until Oscar offered us his plane, I was thinking we could maybe go next weekend. But I think this weekend might be better. We won't get a chance to settle into a routine and then have to disrupt it." He brushed his thumb over her cheek. "Obviously, it's important to us both how Owen will deal with it. But before we even get to him, I need to know how you feel."

She held his gaze for a long moment. She wished she could get lost in his eyes forever. He raised an eyebrow, and she knew he wasn't just asking about a weekend away. He was asking how she felt about them moving to Montana.

She smiled and nodded. She didn't want to say the words out loud just yet, but she wanted him to know that, yes, she loved the idea.

Owen came back out and held up his little plastic volcano with a smile. "Come and play?"

"Sure." Reid took hold of Tara's hand and led her into Owen's room.

Once they were all seated on the floor, he picked up the volcano. "Do you know where there's a real volcano?"

Owen shook his head.

"In Montana, where I have a house. There's a super volcano, in a place called Yellowstone. Do you want to see it?"

Owen nodded.

"Do you want to fly in an airplane tomorrow and go and see Yellowstone?"

Owen pursed his lips and looked at Tara. She smiled and nodded, holding her breath as she waited.

"In an airplane?"

"Yes."

"Okay." Owen smiled. "Go to Montana."

Tara let her breath out slowly. It'd be so much easier if he were looking forward to it.

Chapter Fifteen

By the time they'd put Owen to bed, all Reid wanted to do was take Tara to bed, too. It'd been a great evening. But the part he'd been looking forward to most was still ahead of them.

"Do you want a glass of wine or beer or … anything?"

He nodded slowly. He was tempted to tell her that what he wanted was her—right now. But they should wait a little while, at least, to be sure Owen was asleep. He went to join her in the kitchen. "Do you want a glass of wine?"

She ran her tongue over her lips and nodded. "I do. I'm nervous."

He chuckled. "Nervous? About flying tomorrow?"

"No."

He knew what she meant.

"You're nervous about finally letting me undress you?"

Her eyes widened, and she nodded.

He put his hands on her shoulders and looked down into her eyes. "Are you nervous about spreading your legs wide open for me and letting me taste you? Do you want to know how my tongue will feel on you?"

She let out a low, shaky breath. "I was. Now I'm not nervous anymore—just horny as hell, and you haven't even touched me yet."

He smiled. "Words can touch you."

"I believe yours just did."

"Are you wet?"

She dropped her gaze and nodded.

"Are your nipples hard?" He knew they were. They were pointing at him through her top. He wanted to close his hands around her breasts and feel the hard peaks in his mouth, but since they had to wait a little while before he could, he wanted to make the most of it by touching her with his words.

She nodded again and looked up at him from under her long lashes. "I didn't think you'd ..."

"What?" He smiled. "Just because I didn't rush you into bed, it doesn't mean that I haven't been hard for you every time I've been near you." He took hold of her hand and placed it over his aching cock. "This is what you do to me."

She smiled and cupped him in her hand. "I want ..."

"What?"

He wanted to hear her say it, but she shook her head.

"You want to feel me inside you?"

She nodded. Her cheeks were flushed pink, but it was as much arousal as embarrassment.

"I want to be inside you. I want to feel you under me, your legs spread wide for me, and I want to fuck you hard."

She gasped at his last words and looped her arms up around his neck. He crushed her to his chest as he backed her against the kitchen counter and claimed her mouth. He loved the way she kissed him. It was a taste of what was to come; she was soft and warm and yielded to him as he entered and explored her. But it wasn't enough. He rocked his hips against her. If it weren't for Owen, he'd take her here and now up against the cabinet. No. The voice of reason broke through the thundering of blood in his veins. Not just for Owen's sake, but for theirs too. This first time should be in her bed, naked and not rushed. Well, maybe the second time they could go more slowly. He doubted he'd be able to the first time, and judging by the way she was kissing him and rubbing herself against him, she wouldn't want him to.

"Do you still want that glass of wine?"

She shook her head. "I want you to do what you said."

He rocked his hips, loving the way she bit her bottom lip. He wanted to hear her say it. "You want me to do what?"

"Fuck me hard," she breathed.

His already aching cock strained at her words, eager to oblige. He took hold of her hand and led her to her bedroom. Once they were inside, she turned around to lock the door, and he stood behind her, pushing her skirt up around her waist. It was his first sight of her rounded ass, and he cupped it in both hands, spreading her cheeks wide so he could press himself between them. She moaned and leaned her head back against his shoulder. He needed to get her on the bed.

They quickly and silently stripped down to their underwear, then Reid sat on the bed and patted the space beside him. Tara sat eagerly and reached up to kiss him. She loved the way his tongue felt inside her mouth and couldn't wait for it to be mirrored by the way his cock felt inside her. She was out of control. He'd turned her on so much the way he'd talked in the kitchen. Did she want to know how his tongue felt between her legs? Hell, yes, she did, and even more, she wanted to know how his cock would feel. She clung to him as he unfastened her bra and then moaned as he dropped his head and mouthed her taut nipples.

She reached down and slid her hand inside his boxers, closing her fingers around his hot, hard, shaft. He moaned and sucked hard, making her back arch. In a matter of seconds, their underwear was gone, and he was kneeling above her as she lay on her back. He took his cock in his hand and stroked himself. "Do you want this?"

She nodded eagerly. She wanted him more than she'd ever wanted a man. She held her arms up to him, aching to feel him inside. She didn't want his tongue or his hands; there'd be plenty of time to explore and learn each other later. All she wanted was for him to make good on his word and fuck her hard.

He spread her legs with his knees and lowered himself onto her. She grasped his shoulders as he guided himself to her entrance and rested there for a moment. He was driving her crazy. She needed him to—

"Oh, God! Reid!" she cried as he thrust hard.

She bit down on his shoulder. It'd been a long time for her, and even then, she'd never had a cock like his drive so deep and so hard. It was almost painful—exquisitely, deliciously painful. Her legs quivered as she wrapped them around his, ready to hang on for the ride.

He pulled back and lifted his head to look deep into her eyes. "Are you okay?"

She nodded and bit her lip. Her breath was ragged. It was hard to focus on anything other than the pleasure radiating out from the point where they were joined, the point where his pulsating cock poised ready to stretch and fill her. "Fuck me," she breathed.

He grabbed a fistful of her hair and thrust deep and hard, pulling her head back, so she was looking up into his eyes. He pounded into her, over and over and over again. She clung to his shoulders, moving in time with him, feeling as though he was filling her whole body, her mind, and her soul. She started to moan softly as he took her closer and closer to the point of no return. He smiled and thrust harder as if her sounds spurred him on.

"Come for me, Tara. I need you to come for me."

She nodded and moaned again. She didn't have any choice in the matter. Her inner muscles tightened, and he smiled again. Then he caught her nipple between his finger and thumb and squeezed—hard.

She gasped and let go. Stars exploded behind her eyes as he moved harder and faster, deeper and deeper. Waves of pleasure crashed through her. She was soaring away, and then she felt him tense and grow harder still. He found his release, and it took her to another level. She bit her lip to stop herself from screaming through their frenzied coupling.

He dropped his head and kissed her deeply as she came. He'd done that before when he made her come with his fingers. That had felt like he was claiming her at her most vulnerable. This time, he was vulnerable too. He was claiming her, and at the same time, giving himself to her. A fresh wave of pleasure shuddered through her at the thought that they were claiming each other, and their future.

When they finally lay still, she kissed his shoulder.

He lifted his head and looked down into her eyes and smiled.

"That was …"

"Amazing," she said.

"So much more than amazing."

"You're incredible."

"You are! I've never …" She didn't know how to put it into words.

"I haven't either." He smiled. "I let you down, though."

She shook her head rapidly. "No way on earth could that ever be considered a let-down."

He was still smiling. "You asked me to fuck you."

An aftershock rippled through her. Something about him saying that was just … she shivered. "And you did, well and truly."

He shook his head. "No. I made love to you." He brushed his thumb over her cheek. He looked so serious. She could feel what he meant, and she knew it was true. "I made love to you because I'm in love with you."

She sucked in a deep breath and held his gaze. His eyes looked even deeper green than usual. "You are?"

He nodded.

"I'm falling in love with you, too." She couldn't say she was in love with him. It was too soon. She didn't want to say the words just because she was still high from the best orgasm of her life. She knew she was falling for him. But was she there yet? Probably, but it was something too big to just blurt out because he said it first—and say it way sooner than she'd have expected.

He kissed her shoulder. "Thank you."

She gave him a puzzled look. "For …?"

"For being honest. Just because I've fallen hard for you, doesn't mean that you'll ever fall for me, does it?"

"I'm sorry. I didn't mean to spoil a beautiful moment."

He chuckled. "You didn't. This is me, remember? You're not going to hurt my feelings. I deal much better with the truth. Tell me one thing, though?"

"Anything." She felt terrible. She probably should have just said it, she was at least halfway in love with him, but she hadn't examined it—because she'd believed that it would take a while before either of them wanted to say it out loud.

"Do you think it's feasible? Do you think that it's something you'll want—when you're ready?"

She planted a kiss on his lips. "I do. I really do. You just took me by surprise, and I didn't want to say it back as an automatic response, just because you said it first."

He smiled. "Thank you. And don't look so sad. You haven't upset me. You know I'd rather have honesty."

"I do know. I suppose I'm just used to worrying about hurting people's feelings."

"You'd hurt me more if you weren't honest."

She knew that was true, but the fact that he'd said she'd hurt him more meant that she had hurt him, and she never wanted to do that. She slid her arms around his waist and snuggled into his side. "It's only a matter of time."

He planted a kiss on top of her head. "I hope so."

When he woke in the morning, it took Reid a few moments to figure out where he was. The bed was wrong, the pillow was wrong. Then it came back to him. He was in Tara's bed. He turned on his side to look at her. She was still sleeping. She had the hint of a smile on her face. It made him smile, too. She looked relaxed and happy. He'd like to think he had something to do with that. He knew he at least had something to do with her still being asleep. They'd worn each other out last night.

His smiled faded. After their first time, he'd found himself unable to keep the words in. He'd had to tell her he was in love with her. The way they'd kissed afterward had been so intimate, he'd wanted her to know there was substance to it. He loved her. He didn't know what he'd expected, but it hadn't been for her to tell him that she was falling in love and that it'd just take time. It was good, it was logical and perfectly reasonable, but he couldn't help feeling disappointed. Maybe, given his knowledge of how women and their emotions worked, he'd expected a special moment. Maybe he'd expected her to be thrilled and to tell him she loved him, too. He pursed his lips. She had him turned right around. He didn't need that reaction. He only needed to know that they were on track. That, with time, she'd fall in love with him and the future he envisioned for them would be possible.

They were going to sow the seeds for that future today, by going to Montana. He hoped Owen would do well with it. He slid out of bed. If Owen was going to do well today, then maybe it'd be better if the day didn't start with him finding Reid in his mom's bed. He dropped a light kiss on her hair, not wanting to disturb her and then grabbed his bag and went to take a shower.

Chapter Sixteen

Owen stared out the window of the airplane. His little nose was almost pressed against the glass. Tara hadn't known how he'd react to flying. It wasn't something they'd ever done before. She wouldn't have attempted to take him on a commercial airliner. And she'd certainly never dreamed that they might fly in a private jet. He'd done well so far. It must be the magic Reid worked on him. He'd ridden quietly in the cab to the airport. He'd smiled at Woody, the pilot, when Reid had introduced him. And since they'd been on the plane, he'd spent most of the time staring out the window looking fascinated as he watched the world go by beneath them.

She looked over at Reid, and he smiled back at her. She still felt bad about last night. Well, in a lot of ways she felt great. He was amazing in bed—and out of it. She still couldn't believe how much he'd turned her on just by talking to her first. He'd talked to her again much later. Just as she'd been drifting off to sleep, he'd started to whisper in her ear, telling her what he'd like to do to her. He'd had her hot and wet in no time, and she smiled as she thought about the expression Nicole had used—she had climbed all over him. He'd rolled onto his back, and she'd straddled him and ridden him. Her nipples were still tender this morning from the way he clamped them between his fingers and thumbs as she'd started to come. A shiver ran down her spine. She couldn't wait to get him back into bed. She couldn't wait for everything that was to happen between them. She shot another glance at him. She couldn't wait to tell him that she loved him, but she needed to be one hundred percent sure that she was before she'd say it. There was no rush. Hell, they barely knew each other. She didn't doubt him, and she didn't doubt what was possible between them, but she needed to get there in her own time.

~ ~ ~

Reid looked at Owen in the rearview mirror as he drove east on I-90. "Are you doing okay back there?"

Owen nodded and smiled back at him. "Volcanoes!"

Reid chuckled. "These are just mountains that you can see now; they're not volcanoes."

"Mountains. Big mountains." He didn't seem to mind that they weren't the erupting kind.

Reid wondered if it was a stretch to entice Owen here by making the claim that there were volcanoes. It wasn't as though they were going to see lava spewing into the air. It wasn't a lie; most of Yellowstone was a super-volcano. But it wasn't like the kind in Owen's pictures. He didn't seem to mind either way. He was happy enough with regular mountains.

Tara smiled at him. "How long is it since you've been here?"

"I came for Oscar and Grace's engagement party last year."

"How long since you lived here?"

"I haven't lived here since I left home to go to college."

"Yet you still keep a house here?"

He smiled, realizing he hadn't explained things to her. "Yeah. You know we grew up here. My parents own a large ranch. They parceled off three lots—one for each of us. And we all built houses." He shrugged. "When we were younger, we all used to come up here regularly for weekends and get-togethers, but I guess we drifted apart. Oscar was busy building his empire. TJ was deployed in the Middle East and me …? Well, I guess I was busy hiding on San Juan Island."

"You didn't ever want to live here?" She looked puzzled.

He knew she was wondering why he'd change his mind about that now. "I always thought I'd come back someday. It's a good place, but there are so many places to see and experience. I wouldn't want to spend my whole life living in just one of them."

She nodded, still looking thoughtful.

She might not want to hear it, but he needed her to know. "I always thought that if I had a family, I'd want to raise them here. It's a good environment." He shrugged. "It's a good community. It might be lacking some of the amenities of the city, but I think the values and sense of community it instills in a person far outweigh the convenience of having everything on your doorstep."

She smiled at that. "I agree with you. I told you I'd dreamed about moving to Wyoming. I'd spend hours looking at satellite maps and wondering how it would feel to live fifty miles from the nearest Starbucks."

He laughed at that. "It feels good because you can make great coffee at home here, but you can't clear the night sky in LA enough to see a million stars. You can't quiet the traffic enough to hear elk bugle." He shrugged, realizing that he was waxing lyrical. "Even if there were elk in the city." He turned to look at her. "Do you think living somewhere like this is just a nice idea for you … something that you wouldn't be able to deal with in reality?"

"No!" she shook her head rapidly. "I mean, I wouldn't know for sure until I tried it, but I don't think it's a fantasy. I think it would truly be a better life for us." She reached across and took hold of his hand.

He felt like she was trying to reassure him, that she wanted him, that she wanted to live this life with him—even if she wouldn't say she loved him yet.

He pointed to the south. "That's where we're going; we'll be taking the next exit and then driving down through those mountains into the valley. You'll get your chance soon enough to see if the reality feels good to you."

~ ~ ~

It was almost lunchtime by the time they reached the house. Tara looked around in wonder. She felt as if she'd walked onto the set of a movie. The backdrop of mountains set against a big blue sky took her breath away. The Yellowstone River ran through the property, just below the deck. It was beautiful.

Reid came to stand beside her in front of the floor-to-ceiling windows that framed the view. "What do you think?"

She shook her head. "I'm not sure I'm capable of thought at this point. I'm too blown away. It's fabulous. The view, the house ..." She shook her head again in wonder. "I don't know what I expected, but it wasn't anything near as wonderful as this."

Owen turned around to look up at them with a smile. "Owen's home."

Reid squeezed her hand. She didn't know what to say, to either of them. Owen had decided that Reid was home whenever he came to her place, now he felt like he was home at Reid's place. Could this really be their home? She'd love for it to be. "You like it here?" she asked.

Owen nodded happily. "It's pretty."

"Do you want to see your room?" asked Reid.

Owen reached for his hand, and Tara followed them down a hallway.

Reid pointed to the door at the end. "The master is down there."

A shiver rippled down her spine. The master bedroom, the place where later they'd no doubt have a repeat performance of last night. She loved that idea, and it was the thought she chose to dwell on—rather than think about whether it would become their room. This was all going so fast. She was happy about it, and Reid was amazing. Moving here could be the best thing that had ever happened to her and Owen, but still, it was all happening so quickly. Her heart told her it was okay; she could roll with it and it would all work out. Her head told her that she should hold back, wait to see if there were going to be any red flags or hurdles she wouldn't be able to overcome. Just because she was falling for Reid, and just because Owen was so taken with him, it didn't mean that she could throw caution to the wind. Owen's stability and well-being were at stake, but she couldn't put them at risk—even if being with Reid felt like no risk and all reward.

She followed them into a bedroom and tried to blink away tears. Owen was staring around in wonder. Someone—she'd guess it was Jean—had decorated the room especially for Owen. The theme of the whole room was dinosaurs and volcanoes. The bedding, the posters on the wall, everything was something Owen loved.

He wandered around, touching things—the dinosaur bedspread, the volcano lamp. He went to a toy basket that sat by the window and picked up a dinosaur. He brought it back to Reid with a puzzled look. "You like dinosaurs?"

"Yes."

"Your dinosaur? Your room?"

Reid smiled. "No. It's your room. These things are here for you. To make you feel at home."

Owen looked around again. Then he came to Tara and held up the dinosaur. "Owen's home."

She smiled back and bent down to look him in the eye. "You like it here?"

He stepped toward her and landed a kiss on her cheek. "I like it here." He went back to the basket and sat down beside it.

Tara looked at Reid as Owen started taking out an assortment of dinosaurs. They smiled when he started to line them up in order—from the smallest to the biggest. "Playtime," he murmured to himself.

Reid raised an eyebrow at her and jerked his head toward the door.

She followed him out into the hallway. "How did you get all that stuff here for him?"

He smiled. "After you had lunch with Mom, I told her I wanted to bring you both up here, and she said she'd get a room ready for him."

Tara had to laugh. "That's more than getting a room ready. She's created an Owen-Paradise."

He smiled. "Well, this is Paradise Valley. I'm amazed myself. I didn't know she'd go that far." He looked serious again. "And I hope it doesn't freak you out? I know we're at different places in this relationship. I don't want you to see any of this as bribery or an attempt to win you over."

She stepped closer to him and slid her arms around his waist. "I don't. I don't see it that way at all. I see it as you being the wonderful man that you are, and I appreciate it." She planted a kiss on his lips. "And I don't think we're in such different places. We're on the same path; I'm just a few steps behind you, that's all."

He smiled and lowered his head to kiss her. When they came up for air, he nodded. "That's what I hoped. Do you want to see our room?"

She swallowed and nodded. She did. She had to laugh when she stepped inside. "Let me guess, your mom again?"

He chuckled. "Yeah. I think she may have gone a little overboard in here. I said I wanted you to feel like it could be your room."

"I do, but I couldn't see this being your room." It was a little too bright and flowery for her to believe that Reid would feel comfortable. "I want to feel like I'm in your space, like I'm coming into your world. Not that you're creating a world just for me."

"That's a nice thing to say."

"It's a nice thing to feel. I need you to understand that it's you I'm interested in. Not the life we could have with you. If you wanted to come and live in the apartment with us, I'd be happy. I don't need you to create a new life for us."

He nodded, but something was bothering him.

"What? What don't you like about that?"

He shrugged. "We can talk about it tonight. After Owen's gone to bed."

She made a face. "Why not tell me now?"

"Because it's a conversation that's going to take a while and I want us to be able to sit and talk it through."

"Okay."

~ ~ ~

Owen's eyelids were drooping at eight o'clock. It had been a long, eventful day for the little guy and it had taken its toll. Tara helped him get ready for bed, and then Reid walked with him from his bed to their bedroom. When they were back on

Owen's bed, he asked, "If you wake up in the night, what are you going to do?"

"Get you."

Reid nodded. "That's right. Show me."

Tara smiled at him as Owen got down from the bed and went back out into the hallway. He walked to the master bedroom door and tapped on it before he pushed it open. Once inside the room, he stopped and looked puzzled.

"What's wrong?" asked Tara.

"Reid's room. Where's Mommy?"

Reid smiled when he heard her answer.

"Mommy's going to be in here, with Reid."

Owen nodded. He didn't seem to have a problem with that at all. "Which side?"

Reid went to the bed and patted the right side. The side he had to sleep on. "I'll be here."

Tara went to the other side. "And I'll be here."

"Okay. Night night." Reid and Tara smiled at each other as they watched him turn around and go back to his room.

Just as he was about to get into bed, Reid did it again. "What are you going to do if you wake up in the night?"

Owen pursed his lips, making him want to laugh. The kid obviously believed he knew what to do and he shouldn't have to prove it again. But it was important to Reid. He remembered waking up in a strange bed when the family had gone to stay with some of his dad's friends. He hadn't known what to do or where to go or where to find his parents or his brothers. He'd worked himself into a state and screamed the place down until they came to find him. He didn't want that for Owen.

"What if you need to go potty?"

Owen cocked his head to one side, and Reid had to wonder if that was a habit he'd picked up from him. He turned around and went back to the hallway. The bathroom door was directly opposite his bedroom. He reached up for the light switch and luckily was just able to reach it. He smiled. "Go pee!"

Reid and Tara both laughed as he went inside and closed the door behind him.

"Thanks," said Tara. "You really understand him, don't you?"

"I don't just understand him. I've been there. It makes it easy for me to anticipate things that might crop up and be a problem for him."

She nodded, and they both looked up as Owen came back out of the bathroom. He didn't come back into his room but instead set off down the hall. They followed him back into the master bedroom, and he went to the right side of the bed and patted it. "Reid." Then he walked around to the other side. "Mommy."

"That's right," said Tara. "Will you be okay?"

"Yes. Night night."

Once they'd settled him into bed, Reid poured them each a glass of wine and led Tara out onto the deck. It seemed Montana was doing its best to impress her for him. The moon was full and glinted off the recently snow-capped peaks. Even the river sparkled with moonlight. A million stars dotted the big, clear sky.

She drew in a deep breath and blew it out again. "It's so beautiful."

He went to stand beside her. "You're more beautiful."

She chuckled and rested her head against his shoulder. "Thank you."

He liked that she accepted his compliments. She didn't do what so many other women did and try to deflect them or claim that she wasn't beautiful. He never understood if they were fishing for him to say it again or if they didn't have the self-confidence to accept it. Either way, it wasn't appealing. Tara wasn't like other women he'd dated in any way.

"So ..." She turned to look up at him. "Are you going to tell me why you didn't look happy when I said that I'd be fine if you wanted to come and live at my place?"

"Yes." He went to lean on the railing of the deck, and she came to stand beside him. "I know our circumstances are different. And I'm not trying to win you over with what I can give you."

She looked uncomfortable at that.

"And I know you're interested in me for me, not for ..." He didn't know how to put it that wouldn't sound bad. "Not for anything else. But ... I don't want to move into your apartment, because I don't want you to stay in it."

She gave him a puzzled look.

"Maybe I shouldn't have told you that I love you so soon. Maybe that just complicates things. But if we set that aside, I still want you to leave your apartment. For your sake and for Owen's. Even if you don't want to be with me, then I'd like you to consider coming to live here. It's not Wyoming, but it's close enough."

She shook her head and started to speak.

"Please. Let me finish?"

She nodded.

"Obviously, I hope that you'll want to come here and be with me. But my primary objective is that you and Owen should move away from Mark."

"Why?"

"Because he wouldn't be good for Owen. He'd be worse than not good for Owen. I know you and Mom talked about you moving away and seeing how much effort he'd make to see you both. I'm convinced he won't make any effort at all, and I'm also convinced that that would be best for you."

She held his gaze for a long moment. Maybe he was overstepping. In his experience, women didn't like to be told what was best for them. But he was hoping that Tara already knew the truth of what he was saying.

Eventually, she nodded. "You're right. I wanted to try to keep a bond going between him and Owen. But I've heard a lot about Mark lately that makes me not want him around either of us."

Reid was glad that he didn't have to spell out what he'd heard. "Can we take our time?"

"Of course."

She smiled up at him. "I can't see us living here without you."

He smiled back and chose not to ask why. He hoped that she meant she'd want him to be there with them—not that she couldn't take him up on the offer if they weren't a couple.

Chapter Seventeen

Tara looked back at Owen who was strapped into the car seat in the back of the Range Rover. They'd come from the airport in a rental car, but now they were here they had the use of Oscar's Range Rover. She wondered what Nicole would say when she told her. Her sister had talked about Reid giving her a life to which she'd happily become accustomed, and Tara had to admit that she was right.

She was amazed at how well Owen was doing. She'd worried that he'd freak out about being strapped into a car seat—he wasn't used to them—but Reid had explained its purpose to him when he'd put him in it before they left the airport and he'd been okay with it. Today he'd climbed in there happily enough and let Reid fasten him in for their trip down to Yellowstone Park. He'd slept through the night—much to her surprise, since even apart from being in a strange place, she was sure she must have woken him a few times in the night. Reid had quite a talent for making her moan—and scream!

He smiled back at her and waved his dinosaur—his new favorite, selected from the basket Jean had left for him. She'd have to thank her. "Dinosaur's coming to see the volcanoes."

"Yes, he is." She hoped he wouldn't be disappointed that he wouldn't get to see the kind of volcanoes he expected.

"We're going to see lots of other things, too," said Reid. He'd told her this morning that he planned to show Owen some of the geysers, and hopefully, the water shooting up into the air would distract him from the fact there was no molten lava flying around.

They were all mostly quiet while they drove the half hour down the valley to the north entrance of the park in a little town called Gardiner. The whole drive was spectacular. The road followed the river, and the mountains huddled in on either side. Tara had never seen any place so beautiful. She kept looking back to check on Owen, and he seemed as awestruck as she felt. He just stared out of the window, taking it all in. How amazing would it be for him to grow up here? She blew out a sigh. She loved the idea, but she was a practical soul. Great scenery, big skies, and fresh mountain air would no doubt do him a lot of good, but there were other factors to consider, too.

Reid reached across and took hold of her hand. "Are you okay?"

"I am. This is wonderful. Thank you." She wanted to say so much to him. She wanted to tell him how much she appreciated him and everything he was doing—and trying to do—for Owen and her. She wanted to explain to him what she'd meant last night when she'd said she couldn't see them living here without him: He'd become such a huge part of their lives in such a short time that she couldn't see them living anywhere without him anymore.

She couldn't say any of it with Owen sitting there listening to every word. Tonight, though. Tonight, she wanted to tell him and to show him how much he'd come to mean to her. Lying there in his arms in the early hours of this morning, staring out at the big, star-filled sky, she'd had to admit to herself that she was indeed in love with him. It might not sit well with her practical side, but that wasn't a reason not to tell him.

~ ~ ~

Once they were inside the park, Reid pulled into the parking lot of the gift store at Mammoth Hot Springs. He wanted to make sure they were both okay, and he wanted to get them each a gift as a memento of their first visit to the park together. He questioned his reasoning as they walked across the parking lot. On the surface, it seemed like a sentimental thing to do. However, he wasn't given to sentimentality. He couldn't claim that he was doing it because he knew women liked to receive gifts. Tara wasn't interested in material things; he knew that. The biggest gift he gave her was his connection with Owen. There was no doubt about that in his mind.

He held the door open for them to go ahead of him. Owen clung to Tara's hand and stayed close to her as they looked around the trinkets and T-shirts. Reid surveyed the merchandise, still wondering why this had seemed so important to him. It only dawned on him when he was standing at the cash register, paying for the plastic elk Owen had selected and the T-shirts Tara had picked out. She didn't want to let him pay, especially for the one she'd chosen for him, but he said he'd settle up with her later. He finally saw what he was doing. The T-shirts and the elk would be mementos, yes, but they were also the first things they'd bought together. He knew that whenever he saw them wear the T-shirts, or whenever he wore his, he'd remember this day. Perhaps it was another human instinct that he hadn't known he possessed but had observed in others. Forming a new family unit led to acquiring new family possessions. They may only be small things, but he'd felt the need to get started. He smiled as he watched Tara settle Owen back into his car seat. The rented car seat. They'd need to get him one of his own. They'd have to pick out a car together—even if he wanted to drive his from Washington. It wouldn't be much use here on these roads. They'd need to pick out one for her, too. Hmm. He didn't even know if she drove.

He smiled. He didn't know such a detail about her, yet he was planning to spend the rest of his life with her.

Tara caught his gaze. "What's so funny?"

"Nothing. Not funny, just good. I'm amused at myself and how much I'm enjoying this."

She stepped toward him and slid her arms around his waist. "You are? I didn't know how much fun this would be for you."

"The park is good, but it doesn't do much for me. What I'm enjoying is seeing the two of you experience it and ..." He might as well say it. If it were going to scare her away, they'd be better off knowing that now. "I'm enjoying feeling that we're beginning to build our life together."

She held his gaze for a long moment and then planted a kiss on his lips. "I like that feeling, too."

Reid's heart pounded in his chest as he held her closer. No matter what logic his brain fed him, his physiological reactions told him that it mattered. It mattered very much that she should want the same things he did.

"Kisses."

They both looked at Owen who was holding his arms to them. Reid leaned into the car to kiss his forehead and Owen took hold of his ears and stared deep into his eyes. "Owen loves Reid."

"And I love you, Owen."

Owen nodded happily. "Home now."

"Home in a while; we're going to look around the park, remember?"

Owen nodded again. "Home now."

Reid cocked his head to one side. "What do you mean, little buddy?"

Tara leaned in and looked at Owen, then Reid. She seemed to understand what he meant. Her eyes shone with tears, though her smile told him they were happy tears.

"What's home?" she asked.

"Reid's home." Owen looked slightly irritated, as though they should both understand.

Tara smiled at Reid. "I think he means that you feel like home."

Owen nodded, seeming glad to finally have it made clear. He touched Reid's face and then took hold of his hand and put it on top of Tara's and said it again. "Home now."

Reid didn't trust himself to say anything. It seemed that Owen wanted this as much as he did.

Tara glanced across at him as they pulled out of the parking lot and spoke in a low voice. "Home is his safe place, his happy place. When we have to go out and it stresses him, he looks forward to getting home. When he has to be away from me, we don't need to get back to the apartment for him to feel safe. He just needs to get back to me, then he'll say, Home now."

Reid reached across and took hold of her hand as he drove. He didn't know how to put words to the way that made him feel. He wanted to be Owen's safe place and his happy place. He wanted to be that for Tara, too.

~ ~ ~

It was late afternoon by the time they left the park. Owen had loved every minute of it, and Reid had promised to bring him back again soon. Tara wasn't worried about that. Reid knew that Owen needed promises to be kept, and he wouldn't make one lightly.

She jumped at the sound of Reid's phone ringing. It felt like the real world intruding. They'd been lost in their own little bubble since they arrived here and even more so in the vast wilderness that was the park. The phone was a reminder that their real lives were elsewhere and that they were still waiting for them.

Reid shot her an apologetic look. "Sorry. I need to take it. It's a local number I don't recognize."

"Of course." Tara wasn't sure about the logic behind that, but she was hardly going to tell him not to take it.

He hit the button, and she was surprised to see that he planned to talk on the hands-free system.

"This is Reid."

"Reid. You old devil. It's Shane. Shane Remington. How are you? My mom spoke to yours, and she said you were up here."

"Shane! It's great to hear from you. I was planning to get in touch. TJ told me he'd seen you recently. How are you? And congratulations, by the way."

"Thanks. And thanks for the gift. Cassidy would love to meet you."

"I'd love to meet her, too." Reid glanced over at Tara and smiled. "There's someone I'd like you to meet."

Tara had to smile at the sound of Shane's hearty laugh coming through the speakers. Whoever he was, he sounded like someone she'd be happy to meet.

"I know! Your mom told my mom. It's like we're kids again, you know? That's why I'm calling. I'd love to see you and meet Tara and her boy. If you guys want to come out here, Beau's wife Corinne has a little girl about the same age. So, there'd be someone for him to play with."

Reid made a face. "I don't know, Shane. Owen's like me."

Shane laughed again. "I know. I heard, but then, Ruby's a bit like me—loud and obnoxious. Maybe they'll be as good for each other as we were."

Tara loved the way Reid chuckled. Whoever Shane was to Reid, he and Reid were obviously close. "Maybe. Can I call you back later? I don't know what our plans are yet, or even how long we're staying."

"No plans? Damn! You're sure hanging loose. Call me whenever. I'd love to see you whenever it works for you. If that's next time you're here, that's okay, too. There will be a next time, right?"

Reid glanced over at Tara and smiled. "Yes, there will."

Once he'd hung up, he reached across and took hold of her hand. "Shane was my friend growing up here. I think you'd like him." He chuckled. "He wasn't joking about being loud— he was that big, good-looking, confident, friendly kid who everyone just loved. By the sounds of it, he's still the same and more so now. He's not obnoxious, never was. More like a golden boy."

Tara smiled, wondering how the two of them had become friends.

He anticipated her question. "Our parents know each other, though, now I come to think about it, I don't even know how. They're ranchers. Shane and his brothers were big strong ranch kids—cowboys. Anyway, Shane and I got to know each other because of chess club. I taught him to play."

"Wow. That's so cool."

Reid laughed. "I suppose. He only wanted to learn because a girl he liked was in chess club."

"Ha. That sounds more likely, even from what I just heard of him."

"Yeah. I taught him to play chess, he taught me …"

She looked across, wondering what he was about to say.

"He taught me about girls."

She laughed. Now she had an explanation. The way he was with her didn't fit the preconceived notion she'd had of how a highly intelligent guy like him might be a little awkward around the ladies. He'd had lessons from a cowboy!

He glanced over at her, and he looked as close to uncertain as she'd ever seen him.

"I'm not laughing at you. I think it's wonderful."

"He's been a good friend to me."

"Then we should go and see him."

He smiled. "You'd like that?"

"I would. I think it's time we started meeting each other's friends. Though I'm not sure I want this little Ruby teaching Owen about girls just yet."

~ ~ ~

After they put Owen to bed, they went out to sit on the deck with a glass of wine. Reid felt relaxed and at peace. He'd forgotten just how good this place was for him. He didn't see any practical reason that he couldn't live here. He enjoyed his place at Friday Harbor, but it didn't have anything he couldn't have here.

"What are you thinking?" Tara asked.

"That there are no practical obstacles to me moving here."

"Do you see any non-practical obstacles?"

He smiled. "Not obstacles so much as reasons. I'll have no reason to if you don't want to."

She took a sip of her wine and stared up at the millions of stars twinkling above them. "It's a wonderful place."

He nodded and waited. Usually, a line like that was a stall for time or a lead into facts that would either contradict how wonderful it was or confirm it.

She got up from her place on the sofa and came to him. She dropped a kiss on his lips and lowered herself into his lap. "It's time we talk, isn't it?"

He nodded, not wanting to say that if she wanted to be with him, then he'd be glad to talk; if she didn't, he'd rather not hear it just yet. "What do you want to say?"

"That I love you." She took hold of his ears, just like Owen did and looked deep into his eyes. "I love you, Reid Davenport. You are one amazing, unpredictable, sexy man, and I love you. I wanted to wait. I wanted to be more conventional and make sure that it's not too soon." She shrugged. "But it isn't too soon. I didn't want to say those three words back to you just because you said them to me. I wanted to wait until I was sure and to say them in my own time. This is my time. I love you."

He closed his arms around her and hugged her to him. "Thank you." He knew it was more conventional to say it back. But he didn't want to say it as an automatic response either. He looked up into her big blue eyes and saw apprehension. She was more conventional than he, after all. "I love you, Tara." Her face relaxed. She had needed to hear it. "You've just made me one very happy man. We can take this at whatever pace you want. If you want to stay here and never go back, that's fine by me. And if you want to go back to the city and take a year to plan it all out, that's fine, too." He thought about that for a moment and pursed his lips. "But I hope it won't take a whole year, and if you want to stay in the city for any amount of time, we'll need to find a place to live."

She laughed and buttoned his lips together with her finger and thumb. "Can we forget about the practical details for now? I'd rather spend the time showing you how much I love you—and I won't mind if you want to show me."

He didn't need telling twice. She slid off his lap as he got to his feet. He kept his arms around her as he steered her down the hall to the bedroom. He put his lips next to her ear as they walked. "You want me to show you how much I love you?"

She shivered and nodded.

"With my hands?" He closed his hand around her ass cheek and squeezed. He hoped this was doing as much for her as it was him. His cock was already straining, eager to be inside her again.

He loved the way she bit down on her bottom lip to keep herself quiet.

Once they were inside the bedroom, he closed the door behind them and backed her up against it. Her blue eyes were darker, glazed with lust.

"Or should I show you with my mouth?" He pulled her T-shirt and bra down enough so that her full breast popped out and he grazed her nipple with his teeth.

She leaned her head back against the door and arched her back. It was the perfect invitation for him to thrust his hips against hers, pressing his now throbbing cock into her heat. "Or do you want me to show you with my cock?"

She rubbed herself against him. "All of them."

He chuckled and pushed her skirt up around her waist at the same time as she began to unfasten his jeans. "Maybe this time we should go in reverse order."

She nodded, her breath was coming low and shallow. She knew what he meant and seemed as eager for it to be cock-first as he was.

She pushed his boxers down, and he touched her through her panties; she was soaking wet for him. He loved that she was so turned on by him and eager to make love to him. He tugged her panties to the side and couldn't resist dipping his head to taste her.

She sank her fingers in his hair and pulled him back up to look her in the eye. "Reverse order," she breathed and closed her fingers around him, sending shivers racing up and down his spine. "Not hands, not mouth. This first." She lifted one leg up and curled it around his waist as she guided him to her entrance.

He looked into her eyes as he thrust his hips and they both gasped.

"I love you, Reid," she breathed as they started to move together.

He sucked her bottom lip into his mouth and clamped her leg to his side as he set up a frantic rhythm. He wasn't going to last long, and he needed this to be good for her first. He needn't have worried; she soon started to let out the little low moans that he already knew meant she was getting close. He was too, but he needed more, he wanted to be deeper inside her. He leaned all his weight on her, holding her between himself and the door, then caught her other leg and wrapped that around his waist. Now she was wide open for him, at the height he needed, and thrust deeper and harder, carrying them both higher and higher until she gasped and tensed around him. He bit down on her shoulder as her inner muscles clenched him, taking him over the brink. He came hard. It felt like it started in his toes, a wave of searing pleasure that tore through him and spilled into her. Even his scalp tingled as he gave her everything he had.

When they were finally still, he let her legs down one at a time, then led her to the bed where they lay down face to face.

"I love you."

He brushed his thumb over her cheek. "I love you."

Chapter Eighteen

Tara watched in amazement as Owen took Jean's hand and led her to his bedroom. She'd never seen him this comfortable with strangers before. He'd met Jean before and liked her when they had lunch, but this was the first time he'd met Reid's father, Johnny, and he was just as comfortable with him.

Johnny smiled at her. "He's a good boy, isn't he?"

"He is. Though he isn't normally like this around strangers. I was concerned about how this would go."

Johnny and Jean had come over for lunch. She'd wanted to see them and to thank Jean for getting the house—and especially Owen's room—ready for them.

Johnny smiled. "We have a head start on most people as to how to treat him." He jerked his head toward the kitchen where Reid was busy putting the finishing touches to a pasta dish he'd been preparing for them all. "We went through it with Reid. We made a lot of mistakes along the way—well, I did. But we learned and …" He grinned. "I think he turned out okay."

Tara chuckled. "I'd have to agree with you on that."

Reid turned around and eyed them suspiciously. "Why do I get the feeling that you're talking about me?"

"Because we are," said Johnny. "It hardly takes your level of genius to figure that out."

Reid shrugged and came to stand beside Tara. "Don't listen to him."

She laughed. "I think I need to listen. Your mom and dad did such a good job with you, I can learn a lot from them about raising Owen."

His dad looked serious when he spoke again. "Well, if it's advice you're looking for, I wouldn't hesitate to suggest that you go ahead and move here."

Tara met his gaze. She was surprised that he'd just come straight out and say it like that.

He smiled. "I'm not one to beat about the bush. I say it as I see it. The two of you seem to know that you want to be together. This is, in my opinion, about the best environment you'll find for Owen. So, why not do it?"

Tara shrugged. She couldn't see any reason not to, but she didn't want Johnny to think that she was the kind of girl who'd jump straight in. "I want to, I do."

Johnny smiled kindly at her. "Sorry. I think Jean's a bad influence on me. I don't mean to rush you or to put you under any kind of pressure. I'm just glad to see you both so happy, and I truly believe that Owen will do well here." He cast a glance down the hallway that led to the bedrooms, and they all smiled at the sound of Jean and Owen laughing. "There's no doubt that you'll have a support system here. Jean's already talking about us babysitting once Owen's comfortable with us."

Tara closed her eyes to keep in the tears that were pricking. Johnny looked concerned and held up a hand. "Down the line, sometime. When you both know us better."

She shook her head. "I just can't believe how …" She shook her head again. She didn't know how to tell him just how much it meant to her. "All I'm trying to say is thank you."

Reid slipped his arm around her shoulders and smiled at his dad. "Thanks."

At that moment, Jean came running out of the bedroom giggling as Owen chased after her. Tara couldn't remember ever seeing him play like that, even with other kids. He was giggling as he ran, too.

Jean grabbed Reid's shoulders and hid behind him. "You can't get me now!"

Owen giggled again and walked around Reid, but Jean kept turning him, so he stayed between them.

Johnny squatted down, so he was on Owen's level. "What's going on?"

Owen smiled at him. "Jean's got dinosaur."

Tara couldn't believe it as she watched Jean waggle the plastic creature around the side of Reid's knee. Owen laughed and grabbed for it, and she let him get it.

He grinned up at them. "Owen's dinosaur," he announced before giggling and running back to his bedroom.

Jean looked at Reid. "I'll be back, and I'll be ready for a glass of wine," she said with a smile before she chased after Owen again.

It was hard for Tara to believe that just a couple of weeks ago she and Reid had met because Owen had freaked out over his little cousins taking his dinosaur and wanting to play.

Reid hugged her to his side. "I had a feeling he'd do well with them."

"And you were right."

"I'll bet that babysitting offer is sounding more appealing," said Johnny.

She chuckled. "It is. I don't remember the last time I had an evening out. I can't leave him with anyone."

"You can now." Johnny smiled at her.

"Are we almost ready to eat?" asked Reid.

"I am," said Johnny. "I'm starving."

"Can I do anything to help?" Tara asked. This morning had been full of surprises. Owen was surprising her, and so was Reid. She hadn't expected him to offer to make lunch for everyone—or to turn out to be such a good cook; the pasta smelled wonderful, and it was making her stomach growl.

"No, it's …" He stopped and smiled at her. "Actually, yes. Would you mind setting the table?"

As he showed her where things were kept and she laid the table, she understood. She wasn't a guest in his house. They were becoming a team, working together to get things ready for their guests. His dad went to Owen's room and soon joined in the laughter coming from there.

Reid came and slid his arms around her waist as she was getting forks from the cutlery drawer. "How are you doing?" His warm breath sent shivers down her neck as he spoke next to her ear.

She leaned her head back against his shoulder. "I'm wondering how I got so lucky. You are wonderful. Your parents are awesome. Owen's so happy. And I don't want to wake up from this dream."

He chuckled. "It's not a dream. It's your life now—if you want it."

She turned around and planted a kiss on his lips. "I want it. I want you, Reid. I want us, and yes, I want this life."

"So do I. When do you want to start?"

She met his gaze. She knew he'd love it if she wanted to stay here and never go back, but it wasn't that easy. She might not have much of a life, but she couldn't just walk out on it. She needed to wrap it up. There was the lease on the apartment ... She drew in a deep breath as she realized that that was about it. Her work would come with her. Owen was happier here. She'd miss her sister, but ... She smiled. "We need to go back, but I don't think we need to be there for very long."

His eyes shone with happiness as he nodded. "Let's leave tonight? Maybe we can be back here by next weekend?"

Her heart was racing, but it was with excitement, not apprehension. "Okay."

~ ~ ~

"So, letting you take the plane up there worked out well for you, huh?"

Reid smiled at Oscar. He knew his brother would be happy to take the credit for playing a part in making his and Tara's future come together. "It did, thank you. I shall be forever grateful."

Oscar grinned and swaggered his shoulders. "Happy to help."

TJ shook his head. "Don't go preening yourself. It's all down to Reid. He took her up there, took Owen to see the park. And by the sounds of it, fended Mom off. From what Dad said she practically redecorated your whole house before you got there."

"She did." Reid laughed. "Apparently she raced back up there after she had lunch with Tara last week and started prepping the place for us all to live there. She reckoned she hadn't finished, and we took her by surprise by going up on Saturday, but I don't think I want to know what else she would have done if she'd had more time."

Grace smiled at him. They were all sitting in her office at the center. Reid had come over here today because Tara had to work. She was finishing off editing a book. He'd suggested that he and Owen might hang out, but she'd thought it better to stick to their usual routine. She was right. And he'd wanted to see his brothers anyway and tell them his news. Though, of course, they'd heard it from his mom first.

"So, what's the plan?" asked Terry.

"She has to finish work on this book and then we're going to pack her up and move."

"What about you?" asked TJ.

He shrugged. "I brought everything I need to be away from home for a while. I'm good. I'll go back to the island at some point after we're settled in and move more of my things."

"Spider will be disappointed that he didn't get to visit you," said Grace.

Damn. That was a detail he'd overlooked. That wasn't like him, but under the circumstances, he supposed it was understandable. "He can still go. He can stay at the house. It was more about seeing the islands than seeing me."

"You wouldn't mind?"

"Not at all. He can stay there as long as he likes."

TJ raised an eyebrow at him. "Are you looking for a house-sitter?"

"No. I know he couldn't do that. He has the coffee shop to think about, but it'd be nice to think there'd be someone staying there."

"You should talk him into taking a break and going up there," Oscar told Grace. "That'd be a win-win. He could use some time off. I've never known him to take a vacation."

Grace laughed. "I don't think he ever has. It's not what we do."

Oscar made a face at her. "You do now. I keep asking when we can travel."

She shrugged. "I'm a worker bee, not a slacker."

Oscar looked around at them. "Can one of you help me convince her of the work hard, play hard theory?"

"I say go take a vacation," said Reid. "You deserve it more than most people I've ever known."

"Well, since you say so, I'll think about it," said Grace.

"And why would you listen to him and not me?" Oscar asked indignantly.

She laughed. "Because Reid gets it. You play all the time. Reid has to work till he's done and then take a break. I reckon if he can loosen up enough to take a break with Tara—and to give her a break—then I can probably do the same. And hopefully, persuade Spider that it's vacation season and he should go stay at Reid's house."

Terry grinned at Reid. "You sure seem to be working some magic. You come back into town, and within a couple of weeks, you've changed your life, and you're touching everyone else's."

Reid shrugged. He'd be happy to think that was true.

"What about her ex?" asked TJ.

"It turns out that he's an unsavory character, and now she knows it, she doesn't mind moving Owen away from him."

"And he doesn't have anything to say about it?" TJ frowned.

"He doesn't get a say."

Grace made a face.

"What?"

"I hope he doesn't get a say, but you need to figure out where you stand legally. It's not always straightforward to move out of state with a child. She was married to him, wasn't she?"

"Yes, but they're divorced, and he hasn't had any contact for a couple of years."

"She needs to check her custody agreement."

"Thanks." Reid didn't like the sound of that, but it was something they needed to deal with. He checked his watch. "I should get going."

"Are you going to bring her out for dinner one night?" asked TJ.

"I'll talk to her, see what she thinks. I know she wants to meet you, but I don't know how Owen will deal with it."

"You could come to our place, and we all can hang out by the pool," suggested TJ.

"Maybe. Or maybe you could all come to her place. That'd be best for Owen, but I'll talk to her."

"Don't you sweat it." Terry smiled at him. "You and her and the little one are good, and that's all that matters. Figuring out her ex and introducing her to these guys will all fall into place. Don't stress over it."

Reid smiled at him. Terry was an insightful guy. "Thanks. It'll all work out. I'm sure." He straightened his collar and smiled at the rest of them. "I'll see you soon."

He called Tara on his way back to the apartment.

"Hey. How are you doing?" she answered.

"I'm doing well. I just left the center. Do you want me to pick up anything for dinner?"

"Yes, please. Whatever you like. I was going to go to the store when I finished work, but Nicole came by. She's still here."

"Do I get to meet her?"

"If you want to. She wasn't sure if she should wait or get going before you got back."

He smiled. "I'd like to meet her, if she has time. Oscar and TJ would like to meet you, too."

"I'd like that. We'll have to set something up. But you get to go first. You can meet my sister when you get home."

"I'm looking forward to it. I'll be there as soon as I can."

Tara hung up and looked at Nicole. "He's on his way."

Nicole grinned and clasped her hands together. "I can't wait to meet him. Part of me keeps wondering if you've made all this up. It just seems too good to be true—you meeting a guy who understands Owen—who Owen seems to love! And him being rich and gorgeous and wanting to whisk you away from all this to a better life."

Tara laughed. "You think you're struggling to believe it? Can you imagine how I feel?"

"No. I honestly can't. I can't imagine ever getting that lucky."

"Aww, you lucked out with Steve. He's one of life's good guys."

"I know, but he's no billionaire, is he?"

"Nor does he need to be. That's not what I love about Reid. I love who he is, not what he has."

"I know. I'm only teasing you—but you have to admit, it doesn't hurt, does it?"

Tara blew out a sigh. "It doesn't. I know how lucky I am."

"Well, you deserve some good luck after the shitty hand you were dealt the first time."

"Yeah. I haven't heard from Mark for a while. I'm hoping he's just drifted away again, but I should at least tell him we're leaving."

"Pft! Why? You don't owe him a damned thing."

"Okay. Let's not argue about that." She held her sister's gaze for a moment. "I'm going to miss you. I'm going to miss you just dropping in like this."

Nicole gave her a sad smile. "I'm going to miss you, too, but I'm trying not to think about that. It's a small price to pay for you to get the life you and Owen deserve." She laughed. "Maybe Reid will send a plane to pick us up to come visit you."

"Maybe he will." Tara knew he would. And she knew she'd have to get over feeling guilty about letting him do things that cost so much money.

Owen came out of his room when he heard the key in the door. He grinned at Tara and Nicole and said, "Reid's home."

Nicole grinned at her. "It's so cool to see him like this."

Tara nodded, glad that Nicole was getting to see it. She didn't want her sister to worry about them.

When Reid came in, his smile took her breath away. She really hoped this wasn't a dream she was going to wake up from soon.

"Reid's home!" Owen ran to him, and he scooped him up, sitting him on one hip and shifting the takeout bag to his other hand.

"Hey, little buddy. How was your day?"

"Good day. Aunt Nicole's here." Owen pointed.

Reid came in and smiled at them. "Hi, Nicole. It's good to meet you."

"You, too." Tara could tell that Nicole was taken with him.

He went and set the bag down on the counter in the kitchen and set Owen down, too.

Tara went and put her arm around his waist and kissed his cheek, hoping that might help him feel less under the microscope.

"So, I hear the three of you plan to leave town?" asked Nicole.

"We do. What do you think about it?"

"I think it's wonderful. My only concern is that I'm going to miss them."

Reid nodded. "I don't want that to happen. My brothers come up to Montana often on the weekends. I hope you'll want to?"

Tara wanted to laugh at the grin on Nicole's face. "I'd love to."

"And, of course, bring the girls and Steve."

Tara was proud of him that he remembered Steve's name; she'd only mentioned him a couple of times.

"I will, and sometimes I'll come by myself."

Tara did laugh this time. She wasn't surprised Nicole was happy for her—she intended to make the most of her good fortune, too.

"Do you want to stay and eat?" asked Reid.

"I can't. I should get going. I need to get home and make dinner for the girls. I just wanted to meet you. I've heard so much good about you, but I needed to see for myself."

"I know this must be difficult for you. I promise you I'll take care of them."

"I believe you, but I promise you, you'll have me to answer to if you don't."

Tara wished Nicole wasn't so forthright sometimes, but Reid smiled, and she remembered that was how he liked it.

"I wouldn't expect anything less."

Nicole smiled at Tara. "I wish I could stay and interrogate you both, but I need to go. You call me, okay? And don't you dare think you can leave without a hug."

Tara nodded.

"And you," Nicole turned to Reid. "You get a conditional stamp of approval, but I will interrogate you next time I see you."

Reid chuckled. "I can't say I'll look forward to it, but yeah, it's only fair."

"And you." Nicole bent down and landed a kiss on top of Owen's head. "I'll see you soon, little mister."

Owen smiled at her. "See you soon."

Chapter Nineteen

"Want Reid to stay!" Owen's bottom lip was sticking out, and his chin was trembling as he followed Reid to the front door.

Reid looked at Tara. They both knew what was coming.

Tara closed her eyes and sucked in a deep breath. "Mommy has to work."

Reid felt bad for her. She was almost done with the book she was editing, but the author had rewritten a couple of chapters, and it was making things drag on. She was hoping to get finished today. All he wanted was for them to be done here. To pack her and Owen up and head to Montana. But he didn't want to be selfish. He'd been going out every morning and leaving them to their usual routine. Apparently, Owen was ready for his routine to change.

"Reid can be good. Play quietly," Owen said hopefully.

Tara's shoulders sagged, and she smiled. "Do you want to stay and play quietly?"

He winked at her. "I promise I'll be good."

She chuckled. "Okay, then. I hate sending you out every morning anyway."

He went to her and slid his arms around her waist. "And I hate going. We're going to have to learn to work together in the same house soon."

"I know. I've been worrying about you taking so much time off."

"There's no need. I'm ahead of schedule with the books. I have the next two written and edited, and the release dates aren't until November and January."

Tara laughed. "I wish you could train some of my clients. They tend to be last minute miracles."

He smiled. "We're all different. We work in different ways."

"We do. I'm just glad that the three of us work so well together."

"Me, too." Owen was smiling up at them. He tugged on Reid's hand. "Come play now. Let Mommy work."

Reid brushed his thumb over Tara's cheek. He couldn't wait until they were set up in Montana.

He and Owen had a great morning. They played the getting it wrong game and did some drawing and writing. Then they played a numbers game, and Owen surprised him with just how much he understood. But then when he thought about it, he shouldn't be surprised—he'd been the same at that age. Math had fascinated him. It still did.

He and Owen gave each other a puzzled look when they heard the doorbell ring. Owen got up and went and closed his bedroom door, making Reid smile—that was another thing they had in common.

"I'll get it," called Tara.

Reid was surprised to hear a man's voice. He got up and went to Owen's door. As he opened it, he heard Tara say, "No. Mark! You can't see him. I want you to leave."

He opened the door and stepped out into the hallway and found himself face to face with Mark.

"Who the fuck are you?"

Reid met his gaze coldly. "I'm Reid Davenport. What do you want?"

"So, it is true?" Mark ignored him and swung back around to look at Tara. "You found yourself a rich guy to fuck? That's why you don't want to get back with me?"

Tara looked furious. "Get out, Mark! You can't use language like that in my home. Owen's in there."

"I don't give a fuck. The kid doesn't understand anything I say anyway. He's not right. He's soft in the head."

Reid's fists balled at his sides. His blood felt as if it were boiling in his veins. Mark's words brought back all the taunts he'd heard as a kid. He'd thought he was over all that, but to hear those same names directed at Owen made him angrier than he'd ever felt. "Get out." His voice sounded like someone else's. Mark and Tara both looked at him. He breathed slowly through his nose, trying to calm himself. "Get out, now."

"This isn't your fucking place. You can't tell me what to do. You should get out. You shouldn't be doing her while my son's here."

The laugh Reid let out sounded more like a bark. "All of a sudden you care about your son?"

"What does it matter to you? He's not your son."

Reid shook his head. "I wish for his sake he was."

Mark's upper lip curled into a sneer. "So, you want my kid as well as my ex, do you?"

"Yes. I do. I want to give them a good life."

Mark looked around the apartment. "Looks like you're doing a great job of it."

"This is where you left her. We're leaving here and moving to Montana."

"You're what?"

Tara stepped forward. "I was going to call you and tell you. If you want to see Owen, I'll work with you. We'll figure it out."

Mark ignored her and glared at Reid. "You're not taking them anywhere."

"I am."

"No, you're fucking not. He's my kid. She can't take him away."

Reid frowned. He might be right. Reid didn't know. Grace had said something about not taking a child out of state, but he hadn't checked. Why hadn't he checked?

Mark smiled, sensing he had the upper hand. "That's right. You're going to have to file a court order before you can take him anywhere, and I'm going to fight it and drag it out."

"Why?"

"Because you don't get to just come in and flash your money around and take them away. Why should I stay here with nothing?"

Reid shook his head. He didn't understand people at the best of times, and this wasn't the best of times. How could a man want to make life difficult for his own child and for a woman he'd presumably once loved?

"You need to leave." Tara's voice was shaky.

Mark shrugged. "Okay. I'll go. But I'll see you in court." He slammed the door behind him on the way out.

Reid and Tara stood there staring at each other for a few moments. When Reid gathered his wits, he went to her and held her to his chest. "Are you okay?"

"I think so. I don't know if he's right. He might just be bluffing. I never thought of him having any legal rights. I have sole custody."

"We'll figure it out. I can't believe a judge would make you stay here because of him."

She shook her head. "I don't know. I need to speak to an attorney."

"Don't worry. We will."

He led her by the hand into Owen's room. To his relief, the little guy was sitting on his bed clutching the iPod, holding one of the earbuds to his ear.

"Are you okay?"

He didn't respond, just kept staring straight ahead, moving slightly to the music.

Tara went to sit on the bed beside him.

Eventually, he turned to look at her. "Don't like him."

Reid didn't either.

~ ~ ~

Tara sat back and rubbed her neck. That was it; the book was finally done. She didn't know how she'd managed to concentrate this afternoon after Mark's visit, but she had. And now she was free to focus on everything else.

At least, she should be. She needed to start packing ... or did she? Mark couldn't be right, could he? He couldn't make them stay. Reid had gone out when Owen went down for his nap. He'd said he was going to talk to Oscar and get him to help find a good attorney.

She got up from her desk and went into her bedroom to get the shoebox where she kept all her important papers. She pulled it down from the top shelf in the closet and rifled through, looking for the divorce papers. They were all there. The custody agreement awarded her sole custody. Mark had visitation rights—rights which he hadn't exercised for a couple of years. There was also a child support schedule, which he'd ignored. She couldn't believe that a judge would stop her from moving with Owen—especially when she was moving him to a much better environment. She could and did, however, believe that Mark could tie them up in court proceedings for months and stop them from going anywhere until it was all settled.

She rushed to the phone when it rang, hoping it would be Reid, and also hoping that it wouldn't wake Owen.

It was her sister.

"Oh, hey, Nic. What's up?"

"Nothing's up with me. What about you? I thought you'd be all happy and busy packing. You sound down. What's going on?"

Tara told her all about Mark's visit.

"I told you, he's an asshole!"

"Yeah. I agree." Tara blew out a sigh. "I just hope he can't do it, but the way the courts work, it wouldn't surprise me."

"You need to play him at his own game. If he wants to go anywhere near court over all this, then you need to get real about child support and everything he owes you."

Tara sighed. "That'd all get so ugly, Nic."

"He's the one who's turning it ugly. You just need to toughen up. What does Reid think?"

"He didn't say much. He went to see his brother, to see what attorneys he knows."

"Good. The kind of attorney he can pay for is the kind you need."

Tara nodded. She knew that much.

"It'll be okay, sis. It'll work out. I can't believe your Reid will let that asshole stand in his way. I meant to tell you when I met him the other day I had to agree with you—with what you said the first time you met him, that he was like maybe a spy or something. He's not a big muscle-bound, in-your-face action man type, but there's something about him. He might be a secret ninja or something." She laughed. "Sorry. I'm getting carried away, but my point is that I think Reid is the kind to make problems go away—whatever it takes."

"I hope he can."

"You just wait and see. And in the meantime, don't worry about it. Keep packing. I mean, what else are you going to do?"

"I guess. Thanks, Nic."

After she'd hung up, she went back into her bedroom. Her sister was right. She might as well get on with packing. Even if she was going to be here a while longer, she had plenty of things that could live in boxes in the meantime.

Reid seemed edgy when he got back. He came to her and kissed her, but there was an air of tension to him.

"What is it?"

He gave her a half smile. "I found a lawyer."

"And …?"

"And he said he'd need to see your custody agreement and the terms laid out in that. He needs to talk to you if we want to go that route."

"That route? As opposed to what other route?"

He cocked his head to one side and held her gaze for a long moment. "He suggested another route, one that would potentially be much faster and more straightforward."

Tara couldn't help the laugh that bubbled up. The stress must be getting to her.

"What's so funny?"

"Nothing. It's just that Nic called this afternoon, and she thought you might somehow make Mark disappear. You're not talking about a route like that, are you?"

The corners of his lips tugged up in a smile, but he shook his head. "No. It's tempting, but that's not how I operate." He went and sat on the sofa and patted the space beside him.

She gladly sat and leaned against him. She felt like she needed his support in every sense. "So, what did this attorney suggest? I'm guessing it can't be completely aboveboard if it's so fast and straightforward, and yet you aren't thrilled about it."

He nodded. "It's perfectly legitimate. I like the idea. My hesitation is because I don't know if you will."

"So, run it by me. There's only one way to find out."

~ ~ ~

Reid took hold of her hand. He wanted her to love the idea as much as he did, but he wasn't sure that she would.

"This attorney, his name is Jeff. He's a good friend of Oscar's. Has been for years, that's why he spoke so frankly with me and laid out our realistic options. Basically, unless your custody agreement explicitly states that you can move away from California—and I'm guessing it doesn't because you never imagined that you would—then the agreement needs to be renegotiated. And that could take a while."

"How long's a while?"

"Months."

"And this other route?"

Reid adjusted his collar. He could only hope. "Jeff suggested that since Mark's motivation seems to be pure bloody-mindedness, that he might also be motivated by money."

Tara frowned. "I already don't like this."

"Hear me out?"

She nodded.

"Mark doesn't really want to see Owen—he made that clear this morning. He hasn't shown any interest in being his parent. Yet he still has parental rights."

Tara nodded and waited for him to continue.

He was getting to the important part, but he was nervous about how she'd react. "Jeff told me that it's possible for someone to give up their parental rights—to sign them away if they choose."

"He's hardly going to do that."

"He might."

"Why?"

"If he thought it was worth his while."

Tara frowned and met his gaze. "Worth his while? What do you mean?"

Reid swallowed. He'd danced around it long enough; it was time to say it and see how she reacted. "If we were to offer him money in exchange for his word that he'd leave Owen and you alone in the future. I wouldn't trust his word. But we could pay him to sign consent papers relinquishing his rights."

She stared at him for a long moment.

"If he were to do that, it'd mean, at some point, when you're ready, I'd be able to legally adopt Owen."

Her eyes shone with tears, but she didn't say anything.

His heart was racing. He had no frame of reference to know if her tears were happy, sad, or angry. This wasn't something he could compare to previous experience to make an estimation of how she might feel. He was all the way out on a limb—and afraid it was about to break.

"What do you think?" he asked when he couldn't wait any longer.

"I don't know what to think. I'm conflicted, to say the least. I hate that he can have any power over us—but he does. I don't want him to get a penny, and I don't want you to have to pay. Most of all, I don't want him to have any right to come near Owen—or us—ever again …" She took hold of his ears in the way Owen did and stared into his eyes. "I love you so much for wanting to do this for us."

"I love you, Tara. I want to make him go away. With people like that, money works. And I'll be honest, I love the idea that if we did this, Mark would be out of the picture for good and one day, down the line, I could adopt Owen and really be his dad."

A single tear rolled down her cheek, and she smiled. "You might even love that idea as much as I do."

He cocked his head to one side, trying to make sure she was saying what he thought. "You want to do it?"

She nodded. "I wish we didn't have to, but I think you're right. This is the way to clear our path to the future, isn't it?"

"I believe it is.

"Okay. Let's do it."

Chapter Twenty

Tara opened her eyes and stared up at the ceiling and smiled. She was already used to waking up here. They'd been in Montana for three weeks now, and it just got better every day. She turned her head to look out the window at the amazing view. The sun was just peeking over the mountains on the other side of the valley.

Reid's arm tightened around her waist, then he nuzzled his face into her hair. "Good morning."

She turned over and kissed him. "Good morning."

He propped himself up on one elbow and smiled down at her. "I love you, Tara Wilder."

"And I love you, Reid Davenport."

"Do you love me enough?"

She raised an eyebrow, wondering if he meant enough to have sex with him before they got up. She did love him that much, but she was still wary of Owen coming in and catching them. She didn't like to lock the bedroom door here. He'd settled in better than she could have hoped—and she didn't want anything to set him off and set him back. "Enough for what?"

He held her gaze for a long moment. His eyes were a deeper green than usual, but it didn't look like lust. He shook his head. "I'll ask you again later."

She smiled. He was as wary as she was about upsetting Owen. "I love you enough to make you coffee before I check on Owen. He'll come out when he hears me if he's awake."

"I'll make the coffee. You see if you can get your shower in peace before he's up."

"Okay."

He still had an odd look on his face, and she wondered if he had been talking about a quickie when he asked if she loved him enough. She loved him enough to spend the rest of her life with him.

As she took her shower, she wondered if she'd ever be able to let him know just how much she loved him. She loved him more than she'd believed it was possible to ever love someone other than Owen. Once upon a time, she'd believed she loved Mark. She'd known that wasn't love for years, but since she'd met Reid, she understood that what she'd had with Mark hadn't even been a pale imitation of love. It had been a young girl looking to be loved and a young man who … she let the warm water run down over her face and shrugged. She didn't know what Mark had ever wanted. They'd had fun for a while, but when Owen arrived, the fun had ended. She couldn't be happier that he was out of their lives for good now.

Reid had taken care of all of it. He wouldn't tell her how much he'd given Mark. She wasn't sure she wanted to know. She wished it hadn't been a penny. Reid had convinced her it was the right thing to do when he'd explained how he felt about it. He'd said he didn't see it as giving Mark money; he saw it as investing in their future. She smiled as she remembered the look on his face when he'd told her. "If someone asked me to give them every penny I have in exchange for the chance to build a life with you and Owen, I'd give it to them gladly. That's what this is about. We're not buying him off. We're buying peace of mind for our little family."

Tears mixed with the warm water rolling down her face. He thought of them as family. So did she. It had all happened so fast, but that didn't make it any less real. She was happy. Owen was happier than he'd ever been. He was making so much progress. He loved Reid, and now he loved Johnny and Jean, too. They came over every now and then, and she'd even taken Owen up to their house a few times. He'd been nervous the first time, but after that, he'd been right at home. His world was expanding.

She dried herself down and got dressed. When she went out into the living room, Owen was already sitting at the kitchen table drinking his juice. He gave her a big smile. "Owen loves Mommy."

She went to him and dropped a kiss on top of his head. "I love you, Owen."

"Owen loves Reid. And Owen loves Johnny and Owen loves Reid." He flew his dinosaur around his head in a happy arc. "Owen loves dinosaur and Owen loves Jean."

She laughed. It was wonderful to see him so relaxed and happy.

Reid came and handed her a mug of coffee, and she kissed his cheek. He was the reason both she and Owen were happy.

"Do you have a busy day today?"

She shook her head. "No. I'm almost finished. Do you?"

"No. Just the usual. I wondered, would you want to go out for dinner tonight?"

She set the coffee down and looked into his eyes.

"It's just a thought. Mom asked if we wanted her to babysit."

"Jean's your Mommy," said Owen.

"That's right."

Tara thought about it. The first time had to happen sometime, but was she ready for it yet?

Owen was watching her. "Owen loves Jean."

So, apparently, he thought it'd be okay. She nodded slowly. "We could."

"We don't have to."

She smiled. "I know, but I'd like to." She looked at Owen. Reid had helped her to understand that he did better when he knew what was going on. "Would you like to go and play with Jean while Mommy and Reid go out?"

He nodded happily. "One day I can sleep there."

She stared at him.

"Jean said."

She wanted to laugh. It seemed that Jean had been priming him. She knew how lucky she was that not only had she found Reid, but that he'd brought her into his wonderful family. She loved his parents. She'd met his brothers a couple of times now, and she believed that with time she'd become good friends with their fiancées. That thought gave her pause. Would she be Reid's fiancée someday soon? She hoped so.

"Should I tell Mom yes?"

"Yes." It was just one small word, yet it felt like it marked one giant step forward in their life together. The way Reid smiled told her he saw it that way, too.

~ ~ ~

After they dropped Owen off at his parents' place, Reid took hold of Tara's hand. "Are you sure you want to do this?"

"Yes. I'm nervous as hell. Part of me wants to run back in there and take him home, but I do want to do this." She smiled. "After all this time, I think we should finally go out on our first date."

He chuckled. "Well, then I hope you're not a nice girl."

She raised an eyebrow at him.

"Because a nice girl wouldn't let me drive her out into the mountains and ride my cock in the back of the car on a first date."

She bit her bottom lip and shook her head. "You'd better stop talking like that, or there won't be a first date. I'll be taking you straight back home to bed."

He chuckled and opened the car door for her. "No, I'm going to make you wait. I'm going to take you to dinner—and keep talking like that, so that by the time we leave the restaurant, you'll be begging me."

When he got into the driver's seat, she leaned across and kissed him deeply. "I'll beg you now if you like."

"No, please. I won't be able to deny you if you do, and I really want us to go on this first date."

He pulled out of his parents' driveway and headed south down the valley. This date was the most special one he'd ever been on.

He'd asked for the best table at the Valley Lodge, and they'd given it to him. Even he could appreciate the beautiful setting. The huge windows framed a view of Mount Cowen with the river running just below where they sat.

Tara looked around. "Wow! I feel underdressed. I didn't think there were places like this out here."

He smiled. "Paradise Valley has many facets. It can be whatever we want it to be."

"So I'm learning."

"Do you like it?"

"I love it. I really do."

The meal was wonderful. Tara was different without Owen. He loved her in part because she was such a good mother, but it was tantalizing to see her as a woman in her own right. She was beautiful, and even in the short time they'd been here, she'd grown more relaxed and confident. He was a lucky man, and he knew it.

"Would you like to stay for a coffee or a liqueur?"

She shook her head. "I couldn't fit another thing inside me."

He waggled his eyebrows, and she laughed. "Well, maybe that. Later."

"Okay. I can wait. There's something I want to ask you."

"What?"

His heart started to race and that surprised him. He wasn't nervous. He'd known this was what he wanted for a long time now. He was as certain as he could be that it was what she wanted too.

She was watching his face.

He shook his head. Something about this moment wasn't right. That was all he could take from the way his body was reacting. His heart was hammering in his chest, his palms were sweating. "It's okay. It can wait." It wasn't like him to change his plans, and he'd had this planned for a while. But his instincts seemed to have served him well since he'd known her, so he decided to follow them on this, the most important occasion of all.

He was a little disappointed in himself as they drove back up the valley. He'd envisioned this drive being a celebratory one. He'd thought they'd be heading home to fall into bed to celebrate the next step in their lives. They'd no doubt still fall into bed, but it wouldn't be what he'd thought.

"Tonight was wonderful," she said as he turned off the main road and started down the long driveway that led to his parents' house and then past his brothers' to his.

"It was. Thank you."

She gave him a puzzled look. "Is everything okay?"

"It is." As they got closer to his parents' house, he knew what was wrong. He glanced across at her. "Are you okay with Owen staying there?"

She nodded but didn't speak.

"Would you rather we picked him up? It's not late. I doubt he'll be in bed yet."

The relief on her face gave him his answer even before she spoke. "We could just stop in and see if he's gone down yet?"

He nodded and pulled up in front of the house.

"Is everything okay?" His mom looked worried when she came to the door. She knew what his plan was for tonight.

He gave her a reassuring smile. "It is. We had a great time, but we missed him."

She smiled. "He missed you guys, too. He had a great time, but he hasn't settled down yet. Do you want to take him home?"

Tara nodded. "I'm sorry. It was so good of you."

Reid had to smile as his mom hugged her. "Don't you be sorry. I'm proud of you for going at all. It'll take time, and we have all the time in the world." She shot a look at Reid over her shoulder, obviously wanting to know if something had gone wrong.

He shook his head.

His dad came out in the hall with Owen holding his hand. The little guy looked sleepy, but he smiled when he saw them. "Night night."

Tara picked him up, and while she fastened him into his car seat, Reid's mom pulled him aside and spoke in a low voice. "Is everything all right? It didn't go wrong, did it?"

He shook his head and smiled. "Nothing went wrong. It just wouldn't have been right without Owen."

"Aww." She patted his cheek. "Take them home. And tomorrow I want to hear all about it."

When they got back to the house, Reid carried Owen to his room, and Tara followed. She loved seeing the way he was with her son. She wished Owen was his son, too. And in a way, he already was. The two of them were so similar. Owen loved him more than anyone in the world, except her. There was no question of that.

Once he was tucked into bed, he smiled at them. "Home now."

Tara's eyes filled with tears. He was home now, and she felt the same way.

Reid sat down on the bed and patted the space beside him. She went and sat next to him, and he put his arm around her shoulders. "I feel like I'm home now with the two of you."

Owen nodded and murmured, "Home now."

"Would you like this to be your forever home?"

Owen nodded again. He didn't seem to think that was anything out of the ordinary. Tara did. She turned to look at Reid. "I love you, Tara."

Owen smiled. "Reid loves Mommy."

She had to smile through the tears that filled her eyes as Reid held up a little box to her. A diamond ring twinkled inside it. "You know I'm not the most eloquent man on earth. I don't have beautiful words. But I do have a heart full of love for you and Owen. You two have taught me what love is, and I want to spend the rest of my life loving you both. Will you do me the honor of becoming my wife?"

She nodded as the tears flowed down her face. "Yes. Yes, I'd love to marry you. I want to spend the rest of my life with you. And I promise I'll do my best to make you happy."

"Silly Mommy."

They both looked at Owen.

"Reid's always happy with Mommy."

Reid nodded. "He's right. I am." He leaned in and brushed his thumb over her cheek.

"Kisses."

For once, Tara was happy to just let Owen watch as she and Reid kissed. She loved her little boy, and now she loved a man who loved him, too. She didn't want to hide what she and Reid felt for each other. She wanted Owen to see it and understand it, and hopefully, someday grow up to be like Reid.

When they came up from that kiss, Reid looked deep into her eyes. "That's what I was going to ask you this morning. It almost slipped out. I called you Tara Wilder, and you called me Reid Davenport. I wanted to ask if you love me enough to become a Davenport."

She nodded happily. "I do. I'd love to take your name. Tara Davenport has quite a ring to it. I like it."

"And I love her."

Owen smiled. "Owen Davenport?"

Reid caught her eye, and she nodded. "That would make me very happy."

Reid rested his forehead against hers and looked into her eyes. "Me, too."

Owen took hold of Reid's hand and put it on top of Tara's. Then he rested his little hand on top and smiled at them both. "Home now."

Tara's eyes filled with fresh tears. He was right. They had all found their home in each other;

;

A Note from SJ

I hope you enjoyed visiting with the Davenports. Please let your friends know about the books if you feel they would enjoy them as well. It would be wonderful if you would leave me a review; I'd very much appreciate it.

There are so many more stories still to tell. I hope you'll be as excited as I am to know that the next book I'm working on is Angel and Luke's story which means we're going back to the lake! The pilots at Smoke's flight school are angling for a Summer Lake Flyers series, and there are other characters waiting there too. There is also a bunch of cowboys who are all getting impatient for me to return to Montana. And the country singers want me to go to Nashville, beginning with Autumn and Matt. The older couples are growing impatient, and I've yet to figure out whether they'll end up as a series or as novellas when they get too impatient to wait any longer. The short version is that there are still a lot of stories to come.

In the meantime, be sure to check out my Remington Ranch series, if you haven't already. You can get started with book one, Mason, which you can download in ebook form FREE from all the major online retailers but they are all available in paperback if you prefer.

If you'd like to keep in touch, there are a few options to keep up with me and my imaginary friends:

The best way is to Join up on the website for my Newsletter. Don't worry I won't bombard you! I'll let you know about

upcoming releases, share a sneak peek or two and keep you in the loop for a couple of fun giveaways I have coming up :0)
You can join my readers group to chat about the books on Facebook or just browse and like my Facebook Page.

I occasionally attempt to say something in 140 characters or less(!) on Twitter

And I'm always in the process of updating my website at

www.sjmccoy.com

with new book updates and even some videos. Plus, you'll find the latest news on new releases and giveaways in my blog.

I love to hear from readers, so feel free to email me at AuthorSJMcCoy@gmail.com.. I'm better at that! :0)

I hope our paths will cross again soon. Until then, take care, and thanks for your support—you are the reason I write!

Love

SJ

PS Project Semicolon

You may have noticed that the final sentence of the story closed with a semi-colon. It isn't a typo. <u>Project Semi Colon</u> is a non-profit movement dedicated to presenting hope and love to those who are struggling with depression, suicide, addiction and self-injury. Project Semicolon exists to encourage, love and inspire. It's a movement I support with all my heart.

"A semicolon represents a sentence the author could have ended, but chose not to. The sentence is your life and the author is you."

- Project Semicolon

This author started writing after her son was killed in a car crash. At the time I wanted my own story to be over, instead I chose to honour a promise to my son to write my 'silly stories' someday. I chose to escape into my fictional world. I know for many who struggle with depression, suicide can appear to be the only escape. The semicolon has become a symbol of support, and hopefully a reminder – Your story isn't over yet

Also by SJ McCoy

The Davenports
Oscar
TJ
Reid

The Hamiltons
Cameron and Piper in Red wine and Roses
Chelsea and Grant in Champagne and Daisies
Mary Ellen and Antonio in Marsala and Magnolias
Marcos and Molly in Prosecco and Peonies
Coming Next
Grady

Summer Lake Series
Love Like You've Never Been Hurt (FREE in ebook form)
Work Like You Don't Need the Money
Dance Like Nobody's Watching
Fly Like You've Never Been Grounded
Laugh Like You've Never Cried
Sing Like Nobody's Listening
Smile Like You Mean It
The Wedding Dance
Chasing Tomorrow
Dream Like Nothing's Impossible
Ride Like You've Never Fallen
Live Like There's No Tomorrow
The Wedding Flight

Remington Ranch Series

Mason (FREE in ebook form) and also available as Audio

Shane

Carter

Beau

Four Weddings and a Vendetta

A Chance and a Hope

Chance is a guy with a whole lot of story to tell. He's part of the fabric of both Summer Lake and Remington Ranch. He needed three whole books to tell his own story.

Chance Encounter

Finding Hope

Give Hope a Chance

About the Author

I'm SJ, a coffee addict, lover of chocolate and drinker of good red wines. I'm a lost soul and a hopeless romantic. Reading and writing are necessary parts of who I am. Though perhaps not as necessary as coffee! I can drink coffee without writing, but I can't write without coffee.

I grew up loving romance novels, my first boyfriends were book boyfriends, but life intervened, as it tends to do, and I wandered down the paths of non-fiction for many years. My life changed completely a few years ago and I returned to Romance to find my escape.

I write 'Sweet n Steamy' stories because to me there is enough angst and darkness in real life. My favorite romances are happy escapes with a focus on fun, friendships and happily-ever-afters, just like the ones I write.

These days I live in beautiful Montana, the last best place. If I'm not reading or writing, you'll find me just down the road in the park - Yellowstone. I have deer, eagles and the occasional bear for company, and I like it that way :0)